PORTABLE GHOSTS

PORTABLE GHOSTS

MARGARET MAHY

HarperCollins*Publishers*

National Library of New Zealand Cataloguing-in-Publication Data

Mahy, Margaret.
Portable ghosts / Margaret Mahy.
ISBN 1-86950-570-0
[1 . Ghosts—Fiction. 2. Computers—Fiction. 3. Mystery and
detective stories.] I. Title.
NZ823.2—dc 22

First published 2006
Reprinted 2006
HarperCollins*Publishers (New Zealand) Limited*
P.O. Box 1, Auckland

ISBN 1 86950 570 0

Cover design by Natalie Winter, HarperCollins Design Studio
Typesetting by Springfield West
Printed by Griffin Press, Australia, on 50 gsm Bulky News

CHAPTER 1

THERE he was again! Yes! Sitting in the corner by the dictionaries . . . the corner that always flickered with shadows as light came in through the leaves of the tree outside the window. No doubt about it! There he was again, wearing the old-fashioned blue shirt he always wore, and reading — still reading — always reading — the big, fat book he'd been reading ever since she'd first begun to notice him. No matter how many pages he turned (and over the last two weeks Ditta had watched him turn page after page) he never seemed to be any more than halfway through the book. She stared across the library, her eyes narrowing. For some reason . . . she wasn't sure why . . . the sight of that boy in the blue shirt, bent over his fat book, made her shiver.

But this time, as she stared at him, something happened that hadn't happened before. The blue-shirt boy looked up. Their eyes met. Then he grinned at her. *You can't work me out, can you?* that grin seemed to be saying.

Ditta didn't grin back. Firstly because she was trying to work him out (she hated to think there was anything in the world she couldn't understand), but also because her shivering grew suddenly stronger. The boy in the blue shirt was frightening, and being frightened always made Ditta furious. Frightened and furious! Furious and frightened! Who on earth was he? He wasn't a boy she ever saw in the school playground. Could it be that he loved reading so much he spent absolutely all his time in the school library? But then there were times when he wasn't sitting and reading in the flickering corner, and if he wasn't there, he must be somewhere else. And why — why — was she suddenly feeling so chilly inside her school clothes? Why was she suddenly feeling the world was holding its breath? Why was she feeling that everything was about to change?

'Hey,' Ditta began, nudging her friend Lola. 'Do you feel cold?'

'Cold?' exclaimed Lola. 'No way! It's too hot in here. I should have worn my purple top this morning.'

'Well, I feel cold,' said Ditta, glancing back at the blue-shirt boy. And — there! It happened again. All in a moment the boy had disappeared . . . completely disappeared . . . and his big fat book had vanished with him.

'But it's really warm,' Lola was insisting. 'I wish they sold ice creams in school libraries.'

'Or hot dogs,' Ditta replied. *There just wasn't time for him to walk away* . . . she was secretly thinking to herself, and she moved a step or two so she could check in case he was crouching down between the table and the cupboards under the window, but there was nothing except tiny, dancing shadows. She had been about to ask Lola if she knew the blue-shirt boy — after all, Lola knew everyone. But there was no point in asking questions about somebody who couldn't be seen.

'Coming?' Lola was making for the library door. She'd never been a reader, and this year all she could think about was clothes.

'You go,' Ditta said. 'I'm going to look for . . .' She let her voice trail away. 'I want to ask Mrs Carmody something.'

'Always reading! That's *so* not cool,' said Lola, a little grumpily. 'OK. Catch you later.'

Suddenly Ditta was alone in the main library. The other after-school children had gone home. Mrs Carmody was shuffling and sorting in the little room behind the librarian's desk.

Slowly, slowly she turned until she was looking once more towards that flickering corner. The boy in the blue shirt was back again, his thick book open in front of him.

I must . . . Ditta thought to herself. *I must* . . . though every bone in her body seemed to bend away from the boy and his book. *Go!* Ditta commanded her feet sternly. They immediately did their best to grow slow and heavy, but in the end they had to do what Ditta wanted them to do. She was the boss. So she walked right up to that flickering corner, with shadows diving and dabbing at her eyes.

'I can see you,' she said in a quiet, firm voice.

The boy grinned and shrugged his shoulders. 'I can see you too,' he answered. His voice sounded rusty as if he hadn't said anything for a long, long time.

'Tell me truly,' Ditta asked, 'no mucking about. Are you a ghost?'

'Of course I am,' said the boy. His words sounded as if they were struggling out through a throat filled with dust and cobwebs. 'I thought no one would ever ask.'

'Ditta? Is that you? Can I help you?' It was Mrs Carmody. Ditta turned just in time to see the school librarian come out of her little back room with a pair of scissors in one hand and a roll of sticky tape in the other.

'Sorry!' Ditta said quickly. 'I was just talking to myself . . . reminding myself of a book I want to read.'

'Oh, I certainly understand that,' said Mrs Carmody. 'I do it all the time.'

Ditta looked back at the table but she already knew what she was going to see. Nobody. Nothing and nobody. For the second time in a few minutes the blue-shirt boy had vanished. And now Mrs Carmody sat down behind the desk. Anyone could tell she was going to stay there for a while, so there was nothing for Ditta to do but smile, choose a book and set off for home, leaving school and the library behind her — a library haunted not only by a ghost but by a thousand questions.

# CHAPTER 2

Ditta leapt down the three steps between the library porch and the playground grass, jumping past the climbing plants that scrambled on either side of the steps. And there, straight ahead of her, she saw Max Bryant, the tallest boy in her class, red curls shining out like a torch as he walked towards the school bike stand. Walked? No . . . strange . . . very strange! Max's head was sunk between his hunched shoulders, and his feet seemed to be dabbing at the ground, then quickly shrinking away from it as if a mouth full of teeth might lunge up through the dirt and grass and snap at him. Slinking! Boisterous, bouncing Max — Max who usually bounded by, shouting to people as he bounded . . . Max was actually slinking! Ditta felt suddenly sure that Max was the sort of boy who would be able to see the library ghost. She would ask him if he'd ever seen the ghost and then check up on the reason for after-school slinking.

'Hey Bryant!' Ditta shouted. 'Hang on a bit. I've got something to tell you . . . something really spooky. Something about ghosts.' *That should get his attention,* she thought.

But Max spun around wildly and glared at her. 'Shut up!' he hissed. Then, glancing rapidly from side to side as if the sound of his own hissing had terrified him, he spun around and made for the bike stands.

Ditta blinked with amazement. Why was Max telling her to shut up instead of coming back at her with some smart answer the way he usually did?

'Hey! What's wrong?' she yelled at his back.

'Get lost!' Max muttered, speeding up as if her words were wild dogs at his heels. And suddenly there was Lola again, closing in from the right. She'd been gossiping with the girls who were waiting for the school bus, probably boasting about the new designer T-shirt her mother had bought her the day before yesterday.

'What are you two talking about?' shouted Lola, racing towards them. 'Are you being romantic?'

But Max didn't turn.

'What were you saying to her?' Lola called after him. 'What were you saying that you didn't want me to hear?'

'He was just giving a bit of cheek,' said Ditta quickly. 'You know, joking.'

'He didn't look as if he was joking,' said Lola.

'You couldn't see what he looked like,' said Ditta. 'He had his back to you.'

I'll catch up with Max later, she was thinking. *He won't get away from me. And I'll tell him about the library ghost. He'll end up being really interested. He's that sort of boy.*

In the meantime there was nothing left to do but set off with Lola, listening as she talked about clothes and about a jeans sale in her favourite shop at the other end of town. When they reached the Cinnamon Road corner Lola went one way and Ditta went another, which was just fine. On that particular afternoon being on her own suited her. Max-thoughts and ghost-boy thoughts twisted and twined through her head. She needed to get those thoughts untangled from one another.

But then — watch out, Ditta — there, second house but one, towards the end of Cinnamon Road, leaning on his green gate and enjoying a patch of afternoon sunlight she saw Old Baldy . . . the oldest, most talkative man in town. Ditta studied him anxiously. She mustn't let Old Baldy even begin to discuss anything, not even the weather, for he used such long rambling sentences that listening to a single one from beginning to end was like struggling through a nest of twining vines. *Why do they call him Old Baldy?* wondered Ditta, which was something she couldn't help wondering every time she saw him. Old Baldy's hair was like a curly, white wig and his beard, which was also white, was so full and flowing it looked as if he'd pinned a sheepskin onto his chest.

Quick! Quick! Ditta told herself sternly. *Cross over the road, and look the other way. Stare up into the air. Pretend you can hear a space ship or something.*

'Lovely day!' Old Baldy called after her as she crossed the road, but Ditta just smiled politely and waved and jogged on by, trying to look as if she were late for some important meeting.

Everything's mixed up, she thought. *I have to put things in order. I know! When I get home I'll nip into Dad's office and put it all down in a computer file. There's nothing like a computer for making you think straight.* But then a dreadful thought struck her. She began to run.

'What's the hurry?' Old Baldy was shouting after her. As Ditta began to run she could hear him casting one of his long sentences after her, as if he was a fisherman and she was a clever trout. But she was darting away — off and away — making for home.

Ditta burst in, slammed the door behind her, dumped her bag on the floor just inside the door and raced for her dad's office. But it was just as she feared. Her little sister Mirabel had got home ahead of her and there she was, sitting in front of Dad's computer, peering into the screen as if it was a mirror and she could see her own face reflected back.

'Hey! You had the computer all yesterday afternoon,' Ditta cried. 'It's my turn.'

'I was here first,' said Mirabel.

'It's my turn!' Ditta yelled.

'I was here first,' repeated Mirabel obstinately.

At that moment a new voice cut in.

'Ditta!' called her mother. 'You've dumped your stuff right where anyone could fall over it. How many times do I have to tell you to put your bag and jacket away when you come home? Don't leave them spread across the floor.'

'Nothing's fair!' yelled Ditta.

Yet, oddly enough, now she was home, with her sister refusing to move away from the computer and her mother yelling at her down the hall, Ditta suddenly felt comfortable again.

It was strange to think that being yelled at by your mother could make you feel at ease with the world, but somehow it seemed to work that way. That curious secret worm of fear, which had been crawling through and through her ever since the boy in the library had looked up and smiled, seemed to dissolve away, just as the boy had dissolved.

Fear vanished. She was home. Safe — even though her head was dancing with ghostly question marks. And, suddenly, a surprising idea pushed in sideways through the question marks. It was more than an idea . . . it was an inspiration.

Someone needs to answer strange questions, she thought. *And it could be me. Why not? I could be a detective. I could untwist mysteries and lay them straight. Seven eight! Lay them straight. OK! Where's my bag? Where's some paper? Where's a pen? Here we are. Right! Number one . . .*

She was on her way.

CHAPTER 3

'NUMBER one,' repeated Ditta next morning. She looked sideways at yesterday's notes, then she peered at her reflection, trying to make herself look more detective-like. 'What do you do about a ghost in your school library?' Her fringe was sticking up and out in several directions. She must have managed to sleep with her face in the pillow. 'Behave yourself!' she told it sternly, and raked the comb through it, after which it fell smartly into place. Ditta nodded with satisfaction. Hair should do what a detective tells it to.

She counted on. 'Number two. What's wrong with Max Bryant? I know something's wrong with Max because . . . well, I just know! And number three. What am I going to do about Mirabel? It's creepy having a little sister who spends her whole life crouched over a computer. She should get a life. And number four . . .'

'Ditta,' shouted her mother, 'this is a school day. Get going!'

Ditta dropped her comb and raced out into the sitting room. 'Mum,' said Ditta. 'I've worked out what I'm going to do when I grow up.' There was no use trying to tell a busy mother about a disappearing boy (who might not even exist) but at least she could discuss her future career. Any reasonable mother should be fascinated.

'Tidy your room!' her mother suggested. 'Make your bed!'

'Mum!' cried Ditta, deeply exasperated. 'Not that! Listen! I'm going to be a detective.'

'I made my bed,' said Mirabel in the sort of goody-good voice little sisters can sometimes use. 'I tucked it all in.' She danced from one foot to the other . . . a small, round girl with brown hair, a few brown freckles and brown eyes blinking behind glasses . . . silver-rimmed glasses, quite dashing but smeary.

Ditta shot her a scornful, sideways glance. Mirabel reminded her of a winking walnut with legs and owl eyes.

'Geeky computer nerds like you can't help tucking things in,' she shouted. 'Mum! Listen! I'm telling you something important. I'm going to start detecting today.'

'You could begin by setting up a detective's web page,' said Mirabel, sounding suddenly interested. 'I'll help you.'

But no detective wants to be helped by a little sister.

'I'd set up my own web page if I could ever get anywhere near Dad's computer,' said Ditta. 'But you're always crouched over it like one of those old-fashioned witches crouching over a cauldron.'

Mirabel blinked again. Ditta could see she was quite enjoying the insult.

'Yes and when I'm not sitting at the computer I dance around Dad's office at night chanting spells,' she said, nodding and smiling as she began polishing her smeary glasses for the tenth time that morning. 'You be a detective and I'll be a computer-witch spinning webs like an Internet spider.'

'Ditta! It really nearly is time for you to go to school,' shouted her mother. 'Make your bed and pack your bag. Your lunch is on the bench in the blue plastic box. And be off with you.'

'I'm going now,' said Mirabel in her goody-goody voice. 'I'm ready.'

Ditta ignored her.

'All you ever say is clean up your mess,' she shouted back at her mother. 'I'll never ever try telling you about my plans again,' she cried, diving for her bedroom.

'Tell Max Bryant!' Mirabel yelled down the hall after her. 'You're always trying to impress him.'

On her way to school Ditta had plenty of time to give herself good advice. *Be brave,* she told herself. *Go back to the library after school and try to talk to the library ghost again. He's number one.*

But then, just as she was thinking about the boy in the library (number one), she found herself almost banging into Max (number two) slinking — still slinking — on his way to school. Ditta could tell that whatever it was that had been bothering him yesterday was still bothering him.

'Hey, Max,' she called, and he jumped as if the sound of his own name had terrified him, then tried a bit of speedy slinking to get away from her.

But Ditta wasn't the sort of detective who let herself get lost . . . not this morning. She was beside him in a moment, matching her step with his.

'Hey!' she said, making her voice quieter and kinder. 'Give me a break! Because I know something . . . something way-out strange. And I'll tell you, if you tell me why you're so grumpy.'

Max hesitated, wobbling mid-step. He looked bewildered as if somewhere deep in his head he was riding a dizzy Ferris wheel, and was no longer sure of the true up-ness and down-ness of things. At last he spoke in a mumbling, furtive voice.

'Even if I told you, you wouldn't believe me!'

'I might,' said Ditta. 'Actually, I can believe almost anything. I've had a lot of practice lately.'

Max's eyes swivelled from right to left and then from left to right. Kids everywhere! Everyone shouting at everyone else. Yet, just for a lucky moment, Max and Ditta were moving in a little space that was all their own.

Max made up his mind.

'It's our new house,' he said, still speaking in that unexpected, mumbling voice. 'We've just moved in. We've been there a week. And it's supposed to be a great house — it almost is a great house. Loads of space — and I have a bedroom all to myself with my computer and my mother's aunt's old TV. It's almost like flatting,' he said, sounding a little boastful — more like his usual self. But then he hesitated.

'I can't get anywhere near our computer,' said Ditta enviously. 'My sister's always crouching over it.'

'It's a horror house,' hissed Max in a voice that was soft and fierce at the same time. 'At least my bedroom's a horror room. At night the floor — well, it sort of ripples in the moonlight.

It seethes. And it moans. And I know it's trying to tell me something I don't want to hear, but even if I did want to hear what it's trying to tell me, I can't quite make out the words. And then last night . . .'

Ditta felt her face screwing up in astonishment. Looking sideways at her, Max stopped and screwed up his face too. 'See!' he exclaimed in a despairing voice. 'You don't believe me. I knew you wouldn't. Nobody does. I wouldn't even believe myself.'

'Just because I'm surprised doesn't mean I don't believe you,' said Ditta. 'If something weird's going on I'm allowed to be surprised. Actually I'm surprised because something weird has just happened to me.'

'Hey,' called a voice and there was Lola again. That's the trouble with best friends. They never leave you alone, particularly when they want to tell you about some new pink jeans which fit perfectly.

'Forget it! I'm off,' said Max, and he was.

And then the bell rang. Time to go into school.

I'll catch up with Max after school, Ditta thought.

But even for a well-organised detective, things don't work out quite as they have been planned. There was no point in looking out for Max after school because Lola fastened onto her, talking flat-out, even though Ditta wasn't bothering to be jealous of Lola's new jeans in quite the way Lola wanted. For by now Ditta's thoughts seemed to be seething and hissing like the restless bedroom floor Max had described, twisting and twining like the plants around the library steps. And Max's seething, moaning floorboards were somehow linking themselves to that blue-shirt boy . . . appearing and disappearing . . . flickering with light and shade. *Trickery-flickery!* thought Ditta. 'I'm going to the library,' she told Lola. 'See you later.'

CHAPTER 4

O F course for a while after school there were always other children in the library. Mrs Carmody was kept busy helping them to find the books they needed, as well as piling up books children were returning. As Ditta stepped through the door she thought she heard her teeth chattering. 'Behave yourselves!' she muttered, keeping her words inside her mouth so only her teeth would hear them. She went to stand by Mrs Carmody's desk.

'Can I help you, Ditta?' Mrs Carmody asked.

'I was just curious about something,' Ditta said. 'I was looking around and I began to wonder about the library. I mean, it's rather a funny shape for a school building, isn't it?'

'It used to be a cottage next door to the school,' said Mrs Carmody. She'd been a teacher for a long time and knew a lot of historical stuff. 'But it makes a good school library these days, doesn't it?'

'I might want to be a librarian one day,' Ditta told Mrs Carmody, secretly crossing her fingers — after all, if you were being a detective there might not be enough time left over to be a librarian as well. 'Could I help in the library? Just for a bit. Just to try things out.'

'Great!' said Mrs Carmody. 'I could use a bit of help. Look at all the books the afternoon people have brought back.'

And she began to show Ditta how to sort books and set them out in the right order on one of the library tables before shelving them. Ditta, who used the library a lot, knew most of this already.

'I keep thinking there's someone sitting in the corner over there,' Ditta said to Mrs Carmody, trying out the idea on someone else.

'It's funny you should say that,' Mrs Carmody replied. 'It's a tricky corner, that one. Sometimes, just glancing at it out of the corner of my eye, I've often thought — well, half-thought — there was someone sitting at the table. I suppose it's just the way the tree outside the window casts shadows in that part of the room. Sometimes it can be quite spooky.'

Ditta began shelving the science books. 'Who gave the cottage to the school for a library?' she asked, after a while.

Mrs Carmody looked dreamy and reflective as librarians often do when someone asks them a library question. 'It used to belong to a family called the Saffrons,' she said. 'They lived here for a long time. But then there was an accident and one of the Saffron children was killed . . . a boy. I think he had a fall from the cottage roof. It'll all be written down somewhere. And of course, after that it was all a bit too sad for the Saffrons to go on living here. In the end they gifted the cottage to the school and moved on. A school caretaker lived here for a while. But he didn't stay for very long — I don't know why — I think he found it a bit lonely here on his own. Anyhow, after he left the trustees turned it into the school library.'

She straightened a pile of books. 'Listen, Ditta, I'd love to slip over to the staff room for ten minutes and have a cup of tea. Would that be OK?'

'Oh yes,' said Ditta, being helpful in a deeply sincere way.

As Mrs Carmody walked across the playground to the main school building, Ditta sorted books. Then she shelved them. All the time she was doing this she was plucking up courage, and then — brave at last — she spun round and looked sternly towards the flickering corner.

The ghost was sitting at the table, his book open in front of him. And now, because she was staring at him rather more carefully than usual, Ditta noticed something about him she hadn't noticed before. There was — there definitely was — a faint silvery shine to his edges. She took a deep breath and advanced on him, using the sort of firm steps detectives use in dangerous situations.

'What's your name?' she asked. After all, if you're talking to someone it's useful to have a name to call him by. *But do ghosts have names,* she thought suddenly, *or do they give them up when they become ghosts? Was it polite to ask?*

'Hillarion,' the boy replied, speaking in that rusty, dusty voice. 'Hillarion Allan Longbridge Saffron, but you can call me Hilly. Everyone used to.'

Edging closer to Hilly, Ditta could see the silver light was a true part of him. It not only glowed under his skin but somehow seeped out of him into the library air. And his eyes were silver too, though the pupils were black. He was very pale, which was what you might expect in a frightening ghost, yet somehow merry and cheerful, which was not. His clothes looked old-fashioned without being actually historical. Ditta wanted to ask him if he'd been dead for a long time, but it seemed a private, personal thing to be asking someone you didn't know very well. Instead she asked a question which was almost the same question, but somehow a politer one.

'Have you been haunting for a long time?'

'Years, I think!' Hilly said, and shrugged. 'I really don't know. Every day seems like the first day even though I know it isn't. I think time's different over here.'

'Over where?' asked Ditta, puzzled. 'On the other side of the table?'

Hilly looked puzzled too. 'Partly on the other side of the table, I suppose, but more than that,' he said at last. 'It's just that from here it seems as if we're in different spaces. I mean my space overlaps with yours but it's mainly a different space. No one's ever asked me before, so I haven't really thought about it. And if you don't think about things you don't have the words for them.'

'Am I the only one who can see you?' asked Ditta.

'You see me clearly,' Hilly said. 'Not many people see me as clearly as you. I don't know what most people see . . . an extra shadow maybe, or a sort of shifty, this-way-that-way light.' He shrugged again. 'Seeing ghosts is a special skill. It was great to see you looking at me and know I was being seen.'

'Mrs Carmody almost sees you,' said Ditta.

Hilly frowned. Just for a moment his silver eyes became round and blank like silver coins.

Ditta gasped. She couldn't help it. It was as if the door of an invisible refrigerator had opened somewhere in the library, and an icy breath was breathing out at her. Ditta prickled all over and, looking down, saw goose pimples rising up on her arms. *I'm terrified,* she thought, amazed because she was usually too interested in things to bother with being afraid of them. *This is what terror feels like.* She kept looking down so Hilly wouldn't see her sudden fear. Yet why had those suddenly blank silver eyes frightened her so much? After all, there's nothing scary about coins. You just pick them up and drop them in your pocket.

'That's why I come and go a bit,' Hilly was telling her. 'I don't want the librarian catching on to me. She might try to get rid of me. Spray me with some anti-ghost spray or look up some ghost removal company on that Internet they talk about these days.' He looked over at the two computers in the opposite corner of the library.

'Well, it's hard for anyone in my space to believe we're really seeing somebody in yours,' Ditta said. Her goose pimples were dying away as she tried to make her own attack of fear seem like nothing. 'Are you trying to scare people? Aren't ghosts supposed to be terrifying?'

'I don't know,' Hilly replied, shrugging. 'I mean being a ghost can be a bit of a mystery even to the ghost that's being one. There's nothing peculiar about that. Being a particular person can be a mystery to the person who's actually — you know — being them.'

Looking sideways through the window Ditta saw Mrs Carmody walking back across the empty playground, looking at ease with the world. No doubt she was filled with teachers' tea and biscuits.

Ditta turned back to Hilly. 'Quickly! Quickly!' she ordered him. 'Do you understand everything about other ghosts and hauntings and all that sort of stuff? Being a ghost yourself, I mean.'

'Why should I?' asked Hilly. 'Do you understand everything about other girls?'

Ditta thought quickly. She mostly understood herself, and she could guess about a lot of other girls who more or less matched up with her. But did she understand them? Understanding was different from guessing. Lola, for instance. Lola was her best friend (perhaps) but sometimes she seemed to behave like a best enemy, particularly when it came to clothes.

'I understand some of them,' she said cautiously.

'I think I probably understand some ghosts,' said Hilly. 'But we don't have ghost get-togethers, so I'm not sure.'

Mrs Carmody was now more than halfway across the playground. Ditta had to talk even faster. 'And are you stuck with haunting the library?' she asked. 'You can't — well — walk out of the door and haunt the playground or anything?'

'I don't haunt the library. I haunt the book,' said Hilly. 'I died before I finished it. And now I haunt it. I'm like a sort of bookmark.' He slapped the fat book in front of him.

Ditta gave him an incredulous look. Then she put out her forefinger to touch the book herself.

Hilly's blank silver eyes had terrified her, but it was nothing to the terror that swept through her now. The book looked solid enough, sitting there so comfortably in its thick blue cover. But her finger went through the cover as easily as if the book were made of air . . . different air from the rest of the air in the library . . . different from any air in the true world. Ditta's finger immediately froze just as if she'd plunged it deep into super-cold ice cream made by aliens on one of the outer planets. Ditta snatched her hand back, stared wildly at her frozen finger, then stared at Hilly. Once again the strangeness

— the otherness — of being a ghost seemed to strike back at her. Ditta didn't scream or run away but she'd never been so frightened in all her life.

'Don't be scared. I won't hurt you,' Hilly promised in a soft, urgent voice, 'and anyhow, this isn't the real book. This is just the ghost of the book.'

'Where is the real book?' Ditta whispered. In spite of being so scared she was suddenly sure it was important to find out. Good detectives try to find things out even when they're totally terrified.

But at that moment she heard the library door open behind her. She leapt to her feet, spinning around as she leapt. Mrs Carmody came bustling in.

'Oh, thank you so much, Ditta,' she said. 'I really needed that cup of tea.'

'Great!' said Ditta and glanced back towards Hilly. But he was no longer there.

Was there, perhaps, a faint silvery sheen in the air on the other side of the table? She thought there might be, but then she blinked and the silver sheen (if it really was there) faded quickly, and was gone.

# CHAPTER 5

'Have you got any homework?' asked her mother as Ditta came into the kitchen, home from school at last.

'You always ask about homework,' complained Ditta dropping her bag and jacket on the floor. 'I come in all worn out from being educated and the first thing you ask me is if I've got homework.'

'I like to do a bit of motherly bullying before dinner time,' Mrs Donaldson said. 'I need to keep in practice. So, have you got any homework? Go on . . . you might as well tell me.'

'We've got to do a history project for Mrs Prentice,' Ditta grumbled. She dropped her jacket and pack and collapsed into the nearest chair. 'We've got to choose a partner and work together on it. Just thinking about it makes me tired. And I've got a lot of other things to think of just now.'

'Hey! Put all that stuff away,' her mother cried. 'Don't just sling it all over the floor.'

Ditta picked up her bag and jacket and made for her room. She would spread things around in there. After all, what was the use of having a bedroom if you couldn't spread things around in it?

'How about telling me how pleased you are to see me?' she shouted over her shoulder. 'Just once!'

'I've told you that every afternoon for the last two years,' her mother shouted back. 'You just say "Yeah, right!" and make for the cake tin.'

'Yeah, right!' said Ditta, laughing, even though she didn't quite want to.

The thing Ditta loved about her room was that she could go into it, slam the door after her and slump down. All her old toys . . . all her books . . . all her secrets . . . all the money she had been saving . . . all those notes for the story she was planning to write (once she'd worked out what it was going to be about) seemed to crowd in around her, welcoming her back. When it came to slumping down it was wonderful to slump down in silence and solitude. But today she found silent slumping was going to be impossible.

Mirabel had sneaked into her room ahead of her, and was running her fingers across Ditta's collection of ghost stories.

'What are you smeary-peering at my ghost stories for?' Ditta shouted. 'I don't go through your stuff.'

'Yes, you do,' said Mirabel. 'You spy on me all the time — spy, spy, spidery spy! I just wanted something to read.'

'Well, you're too young to read ghost stories,' said Ditta. 'And anyhow I want to read them myself . . . and not just ordinary reading either,' she added quickly, thinking that reading ghost stories might sound a bit childish for a working detective. 'I need to do ghost research.'

Then Mirabel said something that took Ditta's breath away.

'Are you working on a ghost-boy-in-the-library case?'

Ditta stared at her sister. It was typical of Mirabel to know things she hadn't been told about, but she couldn't have found out anything about Hilly — not even on the Internet.

'Who said anything about a boy in a library?' she asked curiously, too taken aback to be properly cross.

'I saw you talking to him,' said Mirabel.

'But you weren't anywhere near us,' cried Ditta.

Mirabel stared though the smears on her glasses into the space in front of her nose.

'I saw you through one of the library windows,' she said. 'I've seen that boy sometimes when I've been using the library computer. Anyhow I guessed you must be asking him about being a ghost because that's the sort of thing you would be nosy about. Maybe there's a sort of invisible Internet connecting us,' she added, sounding suddenly interested. 'Us being sisters, I mean. Something genetic.' She looked even more pleased with herself for using such a scientific word.

'Yeah, right!' said Ditta, slinging her pack into the corner by her desk and thumping down on her bed. But suddenly she had to talk to someone, even if that someone was a mere nine-year-old computer geek of a sister. 'Suddenly there are ghosts in all directions. You know Max Bryant's family have just had that new house built up on Croyden Hill? Well, he reckons his bedroom floor seethes and moans at night.'

Mirabel blinked behind her glasses. 'Haunted!' she declared. 'It must be.'

'It's a new house,' Ditta exclaimed irritably. 'Ghosts only hang about in old tumble-down places.'

Mirabel shrugged. 'I don't know.'

'I thought I'd go through my ghost books and see if there were any stories about ghosts in new houses,' said Ditta, 'so no sneaking off with them.'

Mirabel's eyes shifted towards her. Ditta could immediately tell, from what she could see of those gingery-brown eyes behind her glasses, that her sister had come up with an idea.

'I know what you should do,' Mirabel said. 'You should ask that library boy. Being a haunter himself he must know a lot about haunting.'

'Yes . . . well, I said there were ghosts in all

directions,' Ditta told Mirabel. 'The boy in the library — his name's Hillarion but we can call him Hilly. A lot of people can't see him.'

'Why can we see him?' asked Mirabel. 'I thought it was me wearing glasses . . . sometimes smears on the lenses can look like ghosts. But he must be more than a smear, because you can see him too.'

Ditta shrugged. She had got over her surprise at having a sister who could see a ghost through the library window, and wanted to be in charge again. 'Most likely we've got special skills,' she said modestly. 'It's probably a talent, like being musical. Hey! It might run in our family. And Hilly doesn't haunt the library. He haunts a book.'

'That book he keeps on reading?' asked Mirabel.

'Sort of,' said Ditta. 'At least . . .' she shivered, and squinted secretly down at her finger. It had been stiff and numb and white, the fingernail blue and bruised, for the last hour and a half. Every time she tried to pick something up it had been as if she were pointing it out to herself first. But now life was creeping back into her hand. She bent the finger cautiously and it seemed to blush a little just around the knuckle. 'The book he's reading is a ghost book,' she told Mirabel. Blinking behind her glasses, Mirabel seemed to think about this.

'He can't walk out of the library,' Ditta went on explaining. 'He has to stay close to the book.'

'Well, that means the book must be somewhere in the library,' Mirabel said, looking even more like a wise, walnut owl.

Ditta realised this was true. 'Why didn't I think of that?' she wondered — but having a finger frozen into a pointing arrow of ice had probably stopped her thinking as quickly as usual. After all, for the past hour she had been frightened her finger might melt. She'd even taken the long way home because it was shady and she didn't want to risk the bright sunlight of Cinnamon Road. Running down Walnut Drive, sliding along Oak Avenue, leaping from the shadow of one tree to the shadow of the next, Ditta had held her right hand protectively over her left one, struggling all the time with her school bag which insisted on sliding down from her shoulder every ten paces.

'I think that book — the one he haunts — must

be in the library,' she said quickly, speaking in a rather louder voice than Mirabel. 'I was just going to tell you that.'

'What was it called?' asked Mirabel. 'Who wrote it?'

'I couldn't see from where I was standing,' said Ditta.

They sat staring at each other. At last Mirabel stirred. 'That ghost . . .' she began slowly.

'His name's Hilly,' Ditta reminded her.

'Hilly,' Mirabel agreed, saying the name as if she were tasting it. 'He always sits in that corner. I've never seen him wandering around the library, have you? I mean he watches the computers, but he's never come over to stand beside them.'

'No,' agreed Ditta quickly. 'And I think that means the book must be somewhere close to where he sits.'

'I was going to say that,' said Mirabel.

'But I said it first,' said Ditta. She closed her eyes picturing the school library. It sprang to life behind her closed lids.

'A corner . . .' she said, sketching the corner in the air in front of her. 'There's a wall full of books . . . reference books . . . dictionaries and encyclopedias and books like that . . . and then . . .', swerving her hands, 'there's the corner. Then there are windows looking out into the yard and all those flickers and flutters of shadow and sunlight. The book might be pushed in with the dictionaries. Only I suppose . . .'

Her voice trailed away.

'Suppose what?' Mirabel asked in a slightly nudging way. Ditta could tell she was trying to keep words flowing between them, knowing that ideas often spring out of shifting words.

'I suppose the book might be somewhere else,' Ditta said. 'It was a thick, blue book. Very old, more like a brick than a book. I did try flipping it over so I could see the cover, but . . .' she shuddered wildly, '. . . it just wouldn't flip,' she finished. 'Anyhow I don't think it was the sort of book Mrs Carmody would have on the shelves. I mean we have a few old books in the school library, but not that old.'

She frowned, picturing the table . . . picturing Hilly sitting opposite her, picturing the book between them. Over his shoulder she could see the window frame and the tree outside the window. Stretching out beyond the tree, she could see the playground with Mrs Carmody hurrying across it towards the library, all warmed up with quick cups of teacher tea. Ditta sat up so sharply her bed bounced under her.

'The stationery cupboard!' she cried.

'What do you mean *stationary* cupboard?' Mirabel said. 'Cupboards are always stationary . . . they don't jiggle around except in earthquakes. Oh hang on! You mean those cupboards where Mrs Carmody keeps paper and stuff?'

'There could easily be an old book at the back of those cupboards!' cried Ditta. 'Pushed right in at the back.' She wanted to search the library cupboards immediately, but knew she would have to wait until tomorrow after school. All the same she felt so excited about being connected to a ghost who haunted a book she longed to go on boasting about it, and Mirabel was the only person she could boast to. Her mother and father would listen to her — they were good that way — but they were parents like Max's parents and would never take a ghost seriously. But Mirabel was still there, listening, and Mirabel was right. Ideas can come from words.

Ditta chattered on. 'It's funny really. I've read about ghosts for years and years but I've never believed in them until now. And suddenly there's a ghost in the library. And suddenly Max is being haunted. Haunting trouble coming double!'

'Maybe the wood they built Max's floor from was too new . . . maybe it hadn't dried out properly,' Mirabel suggested. 'New wood can sort of crack a bit as it stretches itself.'

'It's more than that,' said Ditta. 'It has to be. Because Max was really scared, and he isn't the sort of boy to be scared of a bit of creaking timber.'

Mirabel stared into space. 'I'll tell you what,' she said. 'Tomorrow we'll look in those stationary stationery cupboards to see if the haunted book's hidden there.'

But Ditta wasn't going to let Mirabel take her adventure away from her.

'Tomorrow *I'll* look in the stationery cupboards to see if the haunted book is hidden there,' she declared, as if she were the one who'd thought of it first. 'And I'll ask Hilly if he has any clues about Max's house. You never know. He might be able to tell me how to straighten things out for Max.'

Mirabel didn't say anything more. She could

tell Ditta was growing bossy and big-sisterish once more, so she simply nodded two or three times then strolled casually out of the room, making for their father's computer.

CHAPTER 6

T<small>HE</small> next day school seemed to go very slowly for Ditta. Even the things she usually enjoyed, like art, seemed to stumble along slowly, and any work she tried to do on the historical project dragged into nothing.

Although she did get a chance to catch up with Max at morning break. 'Hi!' she said in a loud voice. 'Have you thought who you want to work with on your history project?' Then she added in a sort of muttering whisper, 'How was your bedroom floor last night?'

'Shut up,' hissed Max as if the air was full of

listening ears. He certainly didn't want anyone to hear a girl asking him about his bedroom floor. But, remembering yesterday, Ditta had cleverly chosen a moment when there was so much going on around them that no one else could possibly be listening in.

'Did it moan and seethe?' she asked, still muttering sideways.

'Leave me alone,' Max said angrily and slunk away. Having been so frightened herself the day before, Ditta could tell Max was angry at being reminded of just how frightening hauntings could be. The memory of her own icy moments with Hilly filled her head for a moment. Though she felt annoyed with Max for being so secretive and stubborn, at the same time she felt really sorry for him.

'Help is on the way!' she shouted after him. Max didn't reply. But then, just before he disappeared through the classroom door, he stopped and looked narrowly back at her. Ditta could tell he was trying to work out if she was serious about being helpful, or just having him on.

The afternoon bell rang. School was over. Mirabel made for home, probably making a few Internet web plans on the way. Lola's mother picked Lola up in their smart blue car and swept her off to shop for new shirts at a mall on the other side of town.

As they drove away, spinning busily out of the school gate, they almost bowled Old Baldy over. He was walking home from the park where he spent his afternoons, feeding the ducks and working on his laptop.

Old Baldy wobbled in the wind as they sped past, then shook the goose-head handle of his walking stick after the vanishing car. Ditta saw all this as she made for the library.

Mrs Carmody was lining books up on one of the tables. 'What? You back again? You must have enjoyed being here yesterday afternoon.'

'I did,' said Ditta. 'Could I do a bit more shelving?'

'I'd be glad of the help,' said Mrs Carmody.

'Sort those books on the trolley by the issue desk.' Then she went to help some little children from the junior school check out their picture books.

The library was always busy for about half an hour after school was out. Mrs Carmody issued books and Ditta shelved. She found she was getting good at it. Every now and then she glanced over at Hilly's corner. Sometimes it looked completely empty apart from the usual shadows, and sometimes the whole corner seemed to take on a curious silvery gleam. Once she definitely saw Hilly sitting there and smiling back at her, but when she looked back only a moment later the corner was totally empty. In between times Ditta slyly studied the cupboards that jutted out from under the windows. There was a display of books about wild animals along the tops of the cupboards, and their doors were tightly shut.

The last child left. Finally there was no one in the library except Mrs Carmody and Ditta. 'I've got time to finish that shelving,' Ditta said quickly.

'Would you mind if I cut across to the staff room to have a quick cup of tea?' asked Mrs

Carmody. Ditta had been sure she would say this.

'No, that's fine!' Ditta cried, sounding a bit too enthusiastic, perhaps, because Mrs Carmody gave her a sudden sharp look. But like all teachers she was desperate for after-school tea. Ditta watched her setting off across the playground, almost running in her teacher's afternoon-tea frenzy, then quickly turned to look at the table in the corner by the dictionaries.

And — yes — there he was. Hillarion Saffron! Softly and silently he had dissolved into the library air from . . . from where? Where were ghosts when they weren't busy ghosting around in the everyday world?

'Hi,' said Ditta. She didn't want to pay him too much attention in case he grew conceited. A conceited ghost would probably be a real pain. Nodding at him, she made for the cupboards below the window. Locked.

'Do you want to look in those cupboards?' asked Hilly's voice behind her.

'They're locked,' said Ditta gloomily.

'Ha!' said Hilly. 'Lucky you know a ghost.' And as he said this he turned into a twist of silver, curled out of the flickering shadows of his corner and in through the keyhole of the nearest cupboard. There was a moment of silence. Then the cupboard doors rattled, trembled, and sprang open.

Boxes of envelopes. Neat piles of paper. Ditta reached in and began feeling around. A silver thread twisted out through the keyhole of the furthest cupboard and back into the library once more.

'What are you looking for?' Hilly asked, putting himself together again somewhere behind her.

Ditta jumped. 'Don't haunt me!' she cried.

'But what are you looking for?' asked Hilly again.

'Your book,' Ditta said. 'You told me you haunted a book. And you seem to be stuck here in this corner. So I worked out that the book you were haunting must be close at hand . . . maybe in here somewhere.'

'Clever-clever!' said Hillarion, looking at her with respect.

'Can you tell me where it is?' asked Ditta.

Hillarion opened his mouth. She could see he was trying to tell her but no words came out. He struggled and seemed to cough. His eyes turned blank and silver. Ditta hastily looked back into the cupboard, and went on searching busily.

'I . . . I can't quite . . .' Hilly wheezed, struggling to come out with something that, for some reason, he couldn't quite say. 'I think ghosts have to keep some parts of themselves secret,' he said at last. 'I think we have to be mysterious against our will. I'll try again.' Ditta watched him battle against something inside himself.

'Warm!' he said at last in a wheezy, choking voice. 'You're getting warm. That's all I can tell you.'

Ditta moved on to the next cupboard. It was filled with old files and boxes with the labels peeling away from them. Quickly she slid her arm in behind them and felt along the back of the cupboard. Something with legs ran across her hand with a trickling tickle of feet.

Luckily Ditta wasn't scared of spiders. She apologised for disturbing it. 'Sorry, spider!' And then she opened the last cupboard. Instruction books for the library computers. And other books — old books.

'Warmer!' Hilly was mumbling behind her. 'Warmer! Hot!'

Ditta leaned sideways and pushed her arm into the blackness at the back of the cupboard.

'Very hot!' sighed Hilly. 'Boiling now!' And there, in the narrow darkness, Ditta's groping fingers closed around something . . . something that felt like a brick. Behind her Hillarion sighed again . . . a sigh of relief this time.

Carefully Ditta lifted the brick out over the computer instruction books. Old. Very old! Thick with dust. Sneezing, Ditta sent the dust flying up around her. Yes again! The cover was blue. But it was a real book this time. Her fingers didn't go through the cover or freeze into pointing icicles.

'Found!' she cried joyously, holding the book high, then spinning around to look at Hillarion who beamed back at her. 'Hey! You haunt the book. Maybe this means that I can carry you around with me.'

'I hope so!' Hilly cried. 'At last! Life is getting more and more interesting every five minutes.'

There was a sound at the door. Hillarion winked out of existence. It was just as if someone had switched him off.

Mrs Carmody stood, looking at the unshelved books with surprise and suspicion. 'You haven't put many of them away,' she said. 'Have you forgotten how to do it?'

'I started reading a book and I got interested in it,' said Ditta quickly, and Mrs Carmody began to look happy, as good librarians do when they hear people have enjoyed their reading.

She relaxed. 'Oh, I know what that's like,' she cried. 'It happens to librarians all the time.' She glanced down at the book in Ditta's hands and her expression changed. 'For goodness' sake! Where did you get that?'

'It was at the back of one of the cupboards,' Ditta said, talking quickly and staring straight into Mrs Carmody's grey eyes. 'I was looking at those animal books on display there, and I suddenly wondered if there were any more books in the cupboards under the display. So I opened one of them and . . . and I saw a spider run in behind some boxes and . . . and I thought the spider should be outside where it could catch flies and . . . and then the spider shot away to the back of the cupboard and . . . and I felt in after it, sort of trying to cup my hand over it, and I trapped this book. So I pulled the book out. And then I got interested in the book and forgot about the spider. And the shelving.' As she said all this Ditta knew she was inventing a story from moment to moment, and yet what she was saying was almost true.

Mrs Carmody looked surprised but she was no longer suspicious. Taking the book she gently slapped its cover. A cloud of eager dust rose into the air and hovered around the book. A few days ago Ditta would have felt the cloud looked a little like a ghost, but now her ghost ideas had changed. Now she thought of ghosts as wearing blue shirts and having strange silver eyes.

'It must have been there for a long time,' said Mrs Carmody. 'I suppose people have found it from time to time but just pushed it into a corner again.' She held it up and squinted at the spine of the book, then opened it and read the title page.

' "Mysterious Hauntings!" ' she read. And then . . . 'It was a present for someone called Hillarion Saffron.' Her expression changed again. 'Goodness! That was the name of the boy who used to live in this house. The one I was telling you about yesterday. The one who fell.' For a moment longer she held the book looking down at it, just a little sadly. Then she patted its cover again. 'Never mind. It was all a long time ago. We should clean this book up and put it into the special reference collection.'

Ditta looked over at the librarian's desk, which was at the other end of the library room. There was a glass case behind it filled with very old books only teachers were allowed to use — though not many of them bothered.

'I wouldn't mind reading this book,' she said.

'Why not?' said Mrs Carmody. 'After all you found it, and the poor old thing will probably enjoy being read again after all these years.'

As Ditta finished shelving the last science books she watched Mrs Carmody carrying the big haunted book across to the library desk.

'I'd better clean it up before you borrow it,' said Mrs Carmody. 'Where are my dusters?' She went through a door behind her desk to a storeroom. Immediately that curious silver writhing began in the air beside the library desk, and Hilly appeared. He seemed pleased to find himself in another part of the library. He grinned and waved at Ditta . . . even danced a few steps, looking as if he were doing something bold and forbidden.

'Fun!' he said. 'Fun! Fun! Fun!'

'What did you say?' called Mrs Carmody from inside the storeroom.

'I said shelving books was fun,' Ditta called back, quickly shelving another book just to prove it. Mrs Carmody came back into the library with a handful of soft, clean rags. Grains of dust rose around her as she dusted the book, hanging in the air, where they glistened and danced like tiny planets. Hilly danced too, turning almost unseen at Mrs Carmody's elbow like a mocking twist of silver in the air, but Mrs Carmody took no notice of him . . . well, almost no notice. Once or twice she hesitated, standing very still as if she were listening to some secret sound.

Shelving in the science section, Ditta managed to pat three books into exactly the right places, while watching Mrs Carmody and the twist of silver, dancing there, and making a few plans of her own.

And at last it was time to go home. Off she went down the steps, her pack feeling heavier than usual because it had the haunted book tucked inside. *Too late to go to Max's house and solve his problems for him,* she thought. *I'll go tomorrow.*

She looked down at the scrambling plants by the library steps and laughed. Suddenly real life seemed like those plants, full of mysterious stories all twisting in and out of each other.

CHAPTER 7

THE next day Ditta didn't go and work in the library after school and she didn't go straight home either. She felt she was in charge of mystery number one . . . well, almost in charge of it. On to the next mystery! Number two!

Free from school and out in the world, enjoying the sunshine, and the distant song of the sea, she ran into the wide arms of a blustering wind which raced towards her, curling and swooping, and wanting to play. It hugged her then raced around her; it snatched up a piece of screwed-up paper from beside a letterbox and tossed it high in the air, juggling with it, then letting it fall away and trundling it off among the leaves.

Ditta felt that if she jumped . . . if she so much as stood on tip-toe . . . she too might be lifted and tossed up and away. But no detective lets the wind think it's the boss of things. Ditta settled her school pack firmly on her shoulders, sure that a pack like hers (secretly weighted down with a blue brick of a haunted book) ought to be too much even for a wild nor'wester.

And as she jogged north, into the wind, with the book bumping at her back, she saw Old Baldy being blown in the opposite direction, billowing back from the park and struggling with his laptop computer which flapped at his side as if it were longing to break away from him and fly off on its own. It was easy to imagine any self-respecting laptop might want to break free from Old Baldy.

But perhaps, thought Ditta, *this wasn't quite fair. Perhaps that laptop was so excited by what he had been telling it that it couldn't help swinging and dancing as it hung from his shoulder.* Though he was on the other side of the street Ditta could see his lips moving.

He was talking . . . talking . . . talking . . . probably trying to control his laptop by tangling it in one of his own serpent sentences. She ran quickly onward, before one of those sentences came twisting across the road to tangle her as well.

Five minutes later Ditta stopped running and peered down into the palm of her right hand, studying the map she had drawn there.

'Croyden Hill. Right,' she said, but turned left, walked a block uphill and then turned again into a street that the hill had curled around itself . . . a sort of cat's tail of a road, so new there was only one house in it. That must be the gate she was making for . . . that very new gate opening onto a freshly laid path cutting through a garden that was only the beginning of a garden. A tall redheaded woman was bending over a spade, thudding it down into soil tough with grassroots, and beyond her Ditta could see the curve of the bay and the white lines of breakers moving into the shore.

'Hello,' Ditta called in a polite voice.

The woman looked up, beamed cheerfully and said a warm 'Hello' just as if they were old friends. She straightened her back and swung the spade back across her shoulder, looking like a noble, pioneering woman in an old painting.

'Max wasn't at school today?' Ditta said, making half a comment, asking half a question.

'He's not very well,' said Mrs Bryant, sighing. 'He's having a day off.'

'Could I visit him?' asked Ditta. 'I'm Ditta Donaldson. I'm in his class at school and I've brought some stuff for him. Homework!' she added, knowing all parents approved of homework.

'Oh, he will be pleased!' said Max's mother. 'Not with the homework, mind you, but he'll enjoy a visitor. He's been pretty miserable all day. Come on in. I'll show you the way.'

So Ditta followed Mrs Bryant up the new path between two rows of new bushes, their garden-centre tags shaking themselves at her like flat, pink fingers. *Take care! Take care!* those flapping fingers seemed to be signalling.

The steps up onto the verandah were so new Ditta felt she ought to walk around them, not on them. All the same, still following Mrs Bryant, she stepped firmly upwards, keeping all that newness in its place, then crossed the verandah and turned in through the front door.

And there she was, inside Max's house, standing in a little hall that smelt of furniture oil and varnish. The floor, beautifully polished, managed to look old and new at the same time.

'Your house looks great!' said Ditta, and she really meant it.

'It's taken us ages to build,' said Max's mother. 'We just love the natural look of this stained wood. Max is up here. This way.'

Ditta followed her up the stairs, sniffing the wood smell and admiring the look of it all. 'Is it oak wood?' she asked.

'Actually, some of it is,' said Max's mother. 'And some of it's native wood from local trees. Totara. Matai. Old wood, but sanded and polished up again. Recycled.' She came to a green door. *Keep Out!* said a notice on the door but Max's mother opened it boldly.

'A visitor for you,' she said. 'Bringing homework!' she added.

As the door swung open, a groaning sound came twisting out to meet them.

Ditta came into Max's bedroom, looking keenly at the floor before she looked at Max himself.

'What are you doing here?' asked Max in a peevish voice.

'Be nice!' said his mother. 'You're lucky to have a visitor. Would you like something to drink, Ditta? Apple juice?'

'That'd be great,' said Ditta, and she meant it. 'Thank you,' she added quickly. (Manners!)

'I'll leave you to tell him about the homework,' said Max's mother. 'Back in a minute.'

Rapidly Ditta studied the newly painted walls, then looked down at the floorboards. There they lay, side by side, floorboard-fashion, perfectly still. There wasn't so much as a twitch.

But when, at last, Ditta looked over at Max, her heart began an uneasy twitching of its own. Max really did look sick — and more than sick. He looked — yes — there was only one way to describe him — he looked utterly haunted. Haunted, pale and somehow shrunken, propped up on pillows. There were books spread across his quilt, but she could tell he hadn't been reading them.

'Have your floorboards been seething and moaning?' she asked in a low voice, perfectly sure he wouldn't want his mother to hear her question.

For a moment she thought Max was going to tell her to get out, or even spring up to push her back through the door. But instead he sighed and wriggled his shoulders deeper and deeper into his pillows. Putting his hands across his face, he spoke through his fingers. 'It was awful last night,' he whispered. 'I told my mother but she doesn't believe me . . . she just says I've given myself bad dreams, and the bad dreams have worn me out. She treats me like a little kid. She says that if I can just get used to my new room I'll get over the nightmares.'

'Parents mostly don't believe you unless you tell them you've done something bad,' said Ditta, staring around Max's room in astonishment. 'Then they believe you straight off. Hey . . . this is a great room . . . apart from the groaning, seething floorboards, that is.'

Max sat up a little higher. He looked around

his room consideringly. 'I'd enjoy it if I could,' he said.

There was a long desk with a computer on it, a printer beside the computer and a bookcase behind it. At the end of the bench was a small television set.

'You've got a computer that's all your own,' Ditta said enviously. 'You'd be able to sneak up here and play games.'

'That computer used to be my dad's,' said Max sounding rather boastful in the old Max way. 'But he had to get a newer, smarter one. This one still works pretty well though. I thought it'd be great, being in here. But now I'm here I just hate it.'

Time to get organised. Ditta opened her pack. She took out the big blue brick of a book and set it down firmly on Max's desk.

'Watch!' she commanded him. 'Look into the air beside that book and see if you can see anything, because if you can . . .'

Max glanced at the book rather scornfully. Then he stiffened. He stared. He sat bolt upright and . . .

. . . and the door opened and Mrs Bryant edged in, carrying a tray that held a plate of biscuits and two glasses of apple juice. She smiled at Ditta and then at Max who blinked at her as she walked across the room and walked right through Hilly who wavered like a boy of smoke and dust, before breaking into wisps and floating in the air around her.

'You don't need to look so amazed,' Mrs Bryant said to Max. 'Your friend will think I've never given you apple juice and biscuits before.'

'No! That's OK,' Max said, still whispering weakly.

His mother looked worried. She laid a hand on his forehead. 'Poor old thing,' she said, while behind her Hilly put himself together, smiling apologetically at Max as he did so.

'Thank you, Mrs Bryant,' said Ditta politely, afraid that Mrs Bryant might stay on, trying to take care of Max. But at that moment the phone rang.

'Oh no!' cried Mrs Bryant. 'There's just too much going on.' And she hurried out, walking back through Hilly and breaking him up into wisps once more. She shut the door behind her.

They were on their own again — Max and

Ditta both staring at Hilly as he put himself together again for the second time in two minutes.

'What . . . what is that?' Max croaked at last.

'Not what, who. It's my friend Hilly,' Ditta explained. 'He's a ghost. I thought he haunted the library, but he haunts that book there which makes him a portable ghost.'

'I think it's because I never finished reading the book,' Hilly told Max.

'And I thought that, being a ghost, he might be able to tell us about your bedroom floor groaning and seething and we might be able to solve the mystery,' said Ditta. 'I thought we . . .'

'You brought a ghost into my bedroom?' hissed Max. 'How could you really, honestly, possibly think another ghost would make me feel any better?'

Hilly looked hurt.

Ditta looked stern. 'It's just like calling in an — an expert. You know, a specialist. You get leaking taps, you call in a plumber. You get a blocked drain, you get a drain layer to fix it,' she said sternly. 'But big deal! If calling in an expert bothers you so much, we'll be off.' She picked up the book, then put it down again. 'I'll just drink this apple juice first.'

'No, no! Wait!' shouted Max. 'Sorry! Sorry! It's just that I —' He looked at Hilly. 'I'm not used to ghosts,' he muttered.

'You get used to them when you have to be one,' said Hilly in his cobwebby voice. He looked around the room. 'Not that I know everything about other ghosts. I mean — I can tell straight off your floor is haunted all right . . . it's got that sort of haunted flavour if you know what I mean . . . but I don't quite know what sort of ghost is haunting it. Did you say it seethes at night? That sounds as if one of us might be trapped in the wood. If I were totally trapped inside my book I'd probably seethe a bit . . .'

Max interrupted him. 'It's more than that now,' he cried in a soft, desperate voice.

Ditta could see her plan had worked. Max suddenly felt he could talk freely to a ghost about his own haunting.

'Much, much more than that. I went to bed last night, and lay there in the dark for a while . . . and then . . .' Max began to shake. His hands on the sheet in front of him began to twist together, and he looked down at them in a sort of scared surprise as if they were doing something without his permission. 'And then it began,' he went on rapidly. 'The floor began its moaning. Light came sort of edging in from the street outside, and I could see those boards down there beginning to twist as if it — as if something were hurting them. And I wanted to call out, but, like I keep saying, it's no use trying to tell Mum and Dad. They think I'm spooked by being in a new house, which I'm not. They stare at the floor but they just don't see it. All they can think of doing is to take me into bed with them as if I was a little kid, and then they spend half the night telling me I'll soon get used to the new house.'

Ditta nodded, remembering that Lola and Mrs Carmody hadn't been able to see Hilly . . . remembering, too, how Mrs Bryant had walked so carelessly through him, breaking him into bits. 'We're the clever ones,' she said. 'We're sensitive.'

'I don't want to be sensitive,' growled Max. 'And it's not their fault. If I couldn't see the things I see, well, I wouldn't believe me either. Anyhow, last night I turned on the light . . . that doesn't altogether stop things but it slows them down and it's more cheerful than the streetlight. And I thought I'd play a computer game. I thought maybe if I had something else to concentrate on, I might be able to — you know — sort of forget about seething floorboards. So I switched on the computer and . . . and . . .' He stopped again, but this time he couldn't go on.

'What happened?' asked Ditta.

Max flapped his hand at his computer. 'Switch it on and see for yourself,' he mumbled and then, lifting the flap of his sheet he flopped it over his face as if he didn't want to see whatever it was that was going to happen next.

'I know a little bit about computers,' said Hilly. 'There weren't any around when I was alive, but I've watched children playing with them in the library.'

Ditta moved to Max's desk. 'I'll switch it on,' she said. She looked at Max. 'Is it haunted?' she asked, but he wouldn't lift an eyebrow from behind the sheet. Ditta switched the computer on. It clicked and hummed in a perfectly usual way. 'It might only be haunted at night,' Ditta suggested.

'No!' Max said, still whispering. 'I tried it

again this morning and . . .' He stopped talking, though his teeth chattered on as if they had little minds of their own.

'Was it on any particular program?' Ditta began.

And then it happened. The whole computer exploded with glaring light. The surface of the screen suddenly seemed as if it had been sucked in on itself. A great gaping mouth snarled out at them while a loathsome glow oozed around the edges of the screen. Ditta found herself looking past gleaming teeth and down a spinning throat, and at the same time she heard the most terrifying sound she'd ever heard. It was almost a moan, but only almost. It was almost a scream, but only almost. The sound was cold . . . so cold . . . and filled with fury and desolation. And somehow within that single voice there was a whole chorus of other voices, all wild . . . all chilly. The room blotted out and her nostrils filled with the smell of something rotting . . . something that knew it was rotting and was furious at its own rot.

Max's voice howled to her from what seemed like another country. 'Switch it off! Switch it off!'

But for a moment Ditta couldn't move. Down below that gaping mouth of a screen she saw fingers crawling like grubs, but Hilly couldn't help either. His hand seemed to dissolve into the computer just as, only yesterday, hers had dissolved into the ghost of the book. Ditta took a breath, then groped around for the control button. Of course just switching the computer off might not be the right way to close down a ghost, but it was all she could think of.

As she scrabbled with her right hand, her left hand accidentally dropped down over the computer mouse, which leapt under her fingers, throbbing like a heart torn out of a living body. But just then the forefinger of Ditta's desperate right hand found the control button on the front of the computer, and pressed it.

Darkness rushed towards her out of that swirling throat. Then the screen's usual reassuring surface came into existence once more, cutting them off from the roaring horrors behind. Light reflected safely from a surface that hadn't been there a few seconds ago. Ditta was back in Max's room, her wild gaze dropping from the computer screen to her left hand (cupped over a perfectly ordinary computer mouse) and then sliding sideways to look at Max, knowing she was just as round-eyed and pale as him.

'Wow!' she said weakly. 'Wow!' And then, 'What is it?' She was shocked to hear how wailing and useless she sounded . . . just as useless as Max had sounded only a moment earlier.

'I don't know!' Max wailed back. 'I just don't know!' Then they suddenly remembered there was a ghost in the room with them. Their heads turned slowly. They both looked at Hilly.

'Oh, there's no doubt it's one of us,' he said in a voice so ordinary and cheerful the eerie room around them seemed to pull itself together, and become ordinary again. 'No doubt at all. I don't know much about computers but I can recognise another ghost when I see one.'

Ditta and Max had both sounded weak with fear, but Hilly sounded interested. 'I'll tell you what I can about this one, and we'll work out what to do next.'

Ditta took a breath. So did Max, who sat on the edge of his bed. Ditta sat on the floor. 'Number one . . .' Ditta began, pointing at Hilly. 'Number one.'

'The room's definitely haunted,' said Hilly, pointing his own finger, but pointing downward. 'You're right. It's the floor . . . the floor is made of haunted wood.'

Ditta peered at the narrow polished floorboards and at the neat skirting, both new and old, at the same time.

'Recycled!' she said to Max. 'Your mother said the wood was recycled.'

Max licked his lips. He was still pale, yet somehow he was already looking a little better than five minutes ago. Possibly he felt better because his haunting was being shared.

'They got it from a special timber yard,' he said. 'A yard that deals in wood from old houses that have been pulled down.' He looked cautiously at Hilly. 'A lot of the wood in old houses is too good to burn or dump . . . so we use it again. That's what *recycled* means.'

'So where did this particular wood come from?' asked Hilly.

Max shrugged. 'Some old house that had been trashed I suppose,' he said uncertainly.

'Well, it's brought a ghost with it,' said Hilly, 'and the ghost was trapped in the wood until . . .' his eye wandered around the room. 'There!'

he cried, pointing triumphantly. 'The skirting board in this room is made of the same wood as the floor. And there's a what-do-you-call-it . . . a power point set in the skirting board. And your computer is plugged into that power point. So I suppose the ghost that haunts the old wood was somehow able to dissolve itself and flow out of the wood and up through the wires, into the power point and then into your computer. It probably wanted a change.'

'But whose ghost is it?' asked Max.

Hilly shrugged. 'I don't know!' he said. 'It was too angry to talk to me. It's so angry words don't work for it any more.'

'Right!' said Ditta firmly. Her own terror was not forgotten but fading. She was already feeling more like her usual self. Something had to be done, and a good detective was probably the one to do it. She looked at Hilly. 'Why is it so angry?' she asked.

'Just because I'm a ghost myself doesn't mean I know everything,' said Hilly. 'But I could tell one thing . . . it's been saving up its fury for more than a hundred years, and its anger has grown more and more powerful as it has grown older.'

'Cheese does that,' said Max. 'Gets stronger as it gets older.'

'Yes,' agreed Hilly. 'Your computer is filled with a sort of cheesy fury.'

'Right!' cried Ditta again. 'Leave it to me. I'll find out. And then we'll get organised.'

'I knew you'd say that,' said Max with a groan, but it was a mock groan this time. Ditta could see something of her bouncing friend coming back into the pale, anxious boy in front of her. It must make a big difference having friends who believed you — who were able to feel what you were feeling yourself (even if one those friends just happened to be a ghost).

'Number one!' Ditta began firmly. 'We ought to find out where this old timber came from. If it's recycled it must have been in some other house before it was in this one. Which house? And number two! Has anyone else been haunted since the first house was pulled down?'

'We got it from that timber place on the edge of town,' said Max. 'You know the one. Woodcraft Timber Supplies. It's got new timber out in front and then at the back there are a lot of sheds and racks of recycled stuff.' He leapt out of bed. 'Let's go now.'

'Hang about!' Ditta protested. 'We can't! Woodcraft's right out on the edge of town. We'd have to bike and my bike's at home. And it is getting a bit late. Tomorrow.'

'But . . .' Max hesitated. Ditta waited.

'I don't want to sleep in here tonight,' Max said at last.

Thinking of that horror twisting and writhing out of the computer screen Ditta couldn't blame him. Even with the computer turned off you would feel it lurking, just waiting to roar and writhe. And, as she thought this, it seemed to her she felt the polished floorboards shift a little — a very little — under her sneakers. Ditta shivered.

'Suppose I invite you round to my house,' she suggested. 'We could be partners on that history project Mrs Prentice set for us.'

Max groaned. 'I haven't got any ideas for the history project,' he complained. 'And there isn't any room in my head for history-project thoughts. Teachers set projects like hunters set traps.'

'But look,' Ditta cried, 'if we say we've got homework we've got to do — homework we've got to do together — my mum would let you come and stay at our house, and your mum might actually let you go, even if you haven't been feeling well. Parents believe in homework even when they don't believe in ghosts. And we've got a spare room. You could stay overnight.'

She thought Max might bristle and rebel at the thought of staying overnight at a girl's house but his face melted with relief.

'Right on!' he said eagerly. 'Let's tell my mum we have to practise teamwork on the history project, and then I'll sling a few things in a bag, because you're totally, dead-on right. Mum will be keen on anything that gets me to do schoolwork.' Max was sounding still more like the Max of those cheerful, bounding days before he had moved into his new house.

And he was right about his mother. Mrs Bryant did look a little anxious to begin with. She put a hand on Max's forehead and peered into his hopeful eyes. But a pleased-mother expression was already creeping across her face at the thought of Max recovering enough to take an interest in a history project.

'I've been worrying about that project,' Max told her. 'Perhaps I've had an attack of homework-haunting. Kids get that some-times.'

'We're supposed to work as a team,' Ditta added quickly, thinking Max's mother might not quite believe in homework-haunting. 'And we have to do research tomorrow afternoon,' she added, winking at Max. 'We'll have to go out to the end of town. So he ought to bring his bike.'

'Right! I'll bring my bike and you bring your book,' said Max quickly.

'It's a big book,' said Mrs Bryant looking at the book with respect. 'A book like that must have a lot in it.'

'It's got more in it than anyone could imagine,' Ditta said.

'This is more fun than I've had for years,' said Hilly and, sliding past Mrs Bryant, he dissolved into the book once more.

Mrs Bryant blinked and shivered. 'Oh, what was that?' she exclaimed. 'It's a lovely warm day but just for a moment I felt as if a cold wind was blowing right through me.' But then she forgot her shivery moment and went to pack clean pyjamas and a toothbrush for Max.

CHAPTER 8

LATER that night Max and Ditta took turns at Ditta's desk and actually did some genuine homework. There was something rather comfortable about doing something so ordinary and working with old-fashioned, reliable pens and papers after struggling with haunted floorboards and a computer that snarled whenever it was turned on. Hilly drifted around the room, studying Ditta's posters with a puzzled expression. Even though he was quite silent it was rather distracting trying to do homework with a ghost in the room. Ditta couldn't stop herself from checking up on him. But then Hilly seemed to grow rather tired of his drifting and folded himself back into the blue book for a while as Ditta and Max read about the early explorers of their own bay.

Croyden Hill — the hill where Max lived — had been named after the captain of the very first ship that had anchored offshore. Just getting from the seashore to the hill had been quite an adventure back then. As they discussed it, quite enjoying themselves, Hilly curled up out of the book once more, and began drifting in between them and reading over their shoulders. You would think a ghost might be useful when it came to history projects but Hilly wasn't much help.

'That was all before my time,' he said rather loftily when Ditta asked him. 'I might be old-fashioned, but I'm not as old-fashioned as that.'

Night fell. Darkness came, and in the middle of the darkness (and in the middle of town) midnight struck on the town clock. Tomorrow somersaulted backwards and suddenly became today.

Ditta and Max set off on their bikes, Ditta carrying the blue book in her pack.

'When you ride down Cinnamon Road pedal quickly,' Ditta warned Max, which was a mistake. Max was feeling so much better he didn't want anyone telling him what to do.

'We're not late,' he said, 'and I want to look around. I'll walk for a bit.'

'Don't!' Ditta cried. 'It's too dangerous.' But her warning fell on deaf ears. Max began strolling along, pushing his bike and then, suddenly, all within a moment Old Baldy was there, leaning over his green gate with his granddaughter, Mrs Marrell, at his elbow, nagging him and trying to brush him down at the same time. Old Baldy began waving at them and trying to lasso them with one of his serpent sentences. Ditta was good at slipping away, waving and smiling, but Max hesitated and in the next moment he was a prisoner.

'Hello there!' cried Old Baldy. 'On your way to school are you? Something I'm glad I don't have to do any more, what with me being the age I am, which is ninety-three — or is it ninety-four — because I find it hard to be sure, what with the years running into each other a bit, the way they do when you get to my age, which as I mentioned earlier, is over ninety and that's an age worth thinking about when you get to it, though, mind you, I'm not one of those stick-in-the-mud sort of pensioners, wandering about, lost in the past, since I've made it my business to keep up with things in a lot of ways, and (you might not think it to look at me) I'm up with the world and all its technology, being a man who has one of those . . . what do they call them? Laptops! Yes! See? I've got it right here, slung over my shoulder . . . one of those portable, carry-around laptop computers, which are very modern one way and another, and I can slip a disk into it and play games . . . (solitaire is one, not to mention a lot of others) or set down my thoughts and memories and save them by pressing the right key . . . and I can receive what they call email on it, having an email address just as if I was twenty-one . . .'

But at this point his granddaughter interrupted him.

'Oh, don't run on like that, Dad, it's bad for you to talk too much not even stopping to take a breath the way you should, because a man of ninety needs to breathe regularly . . . in out, in out . . . without choking himself up with words, talking to someone who'll be late for school if he stops to listen to you, even for a minute, and he probably doesn't want to listen anyway, because anyone can tell at a glance he knows more about computers the way kids do these days than you'll ever know, not even if you were to read the handbook, which you haven't done, have you, even though it's been sitting around on the table for ages . . .'

'Lovely day,' cried Ditta, waving to them both, and slipping skilfully in and out of their serpent sentences, which suddenly reminded her of those plants growing on either side of the library steps. 'Come on, Max, we'll be late for school.' And she nudged Max's bike with hers in such a way that he had to push forward, while Old Baldy shouted after them and Mrs Marrell shouted at Old Baldy.

When Max got onto his bike again his front wheel wobbled with the surprise of it all. But then he pulled himself together and he and Ditta shot away, leaving the commotion behind.

Once in the playground Max leapt from his bike and turned to Ditta. 'Here comes Lola. See you in the park after school!' he said, and went off to the bike stands at the south end of the school grounds. Ditta turned north and almost ran into Lola who was, indeed, charging towards her.

'Oh ho! Is he your boyfriend?' Lola shouted to Ditta in a meaningful voice.

'I just helped him out with a bit of homework,' said Ditta quickly, which wasn't quite true. Max had turned out to be particularly good at spelling, and he had helped her rather more than she had helped him.

'Well, that *is* better,' said her teacher, Mrs Prentice, looking over her pages. 'It was nice to be able to sweep through today's story instead of falling over every second word.'

Ditta looked sideways at Max, who smirked at her. By now it was quite hard to remember yesterday's Max, cowering in his haunted bedroom. And, though it was easy to remember that horrible mouth howling from his computer screen (it was the sort of thing that stuck in your memory forever) it was hard to actually believe in it.

After school Ditta and Lola walked together to the corner, Ditta pushing her bike.

'What did you bring your bike for?' asked Lola suspiciously. 'You don't need a bike. Your house is just down Cinnamon Road.'

'Can if I want to,' said Ditta. 'Anyhow, I might want to go home by the river road.'

'But that's much further,' cried Lola. 'That's mad.'

'I need the exercise,' said Ditta. 'I want to lose a bit of weight.' And Lola fell silent. After all she lived in a house full of older sisters, all dieting and exercising. She couldn't argue with anyone who said they wanted to lose weight.

CHAPTER 9

A T the next corner Lola went one way and Ditta went another. Once she was really on her own Ditta leapt onto her faithful bike, shot down the main road and then turned left onto the cycle track through the park. Max was waiting by the bus stop with his own bike at the ready. Ditta shot by, giving him a mocking wave. But all in a minute Max was after her, and they sped across the park, through patches of light, patches of shade. On their right people walked dogs and fed ducks . . . on their left a cricket team was practising. Ditta could hear the coach shouting at the players. The road curved out around a small lake filled with more ducks and a lot of water plants.

And there, sure enough, was Old Baldy, sitting in one of the green park seats, his laptop open on his knee. His white hair and billowing beard made him look like a sort of shabby, comfortable Santa Claus checking lists of good children and bad children on his computer — but a Santa Claus dressed in brown, enjoying a summer holiday from snow and reindeer. Ditta and Max waved to him, then quickly swung out of the park into a long, straggling street crowded with houses. Small shops stood out like commas in a long sentence and a distant service station loomed at the end like a full stop, with petrol pumps lined in front of it like a row of exclamation marks. It must have been the only street in town with such good punctuation.

Ditta and Max reached the service station safely, then turned very carefully into a road that was busy in a different way. Loaded trucks roared by. Houses stopped crowding one another and spread apart, looking rather more unsure of themselves, as if they had wandered into the wrong part of town. Businesses boldly elbowed their way in between the houses. Ditta and Max passed a second-hand car yard, filled with cars (each with a notice on its front window saying what a bargain it was), then shot by a carrier's yard filled with more trucks and with men pushing trolleys loaded with cartons, or lifting containers on hoists.

'There!' shouted Max flapping his hand. 'There it is!' And he was right. There at last was a long sign saying *Woodcraft Timber Supplies*. An office with a big glass window looked out onto the road while, just beyond the office, a wide gateway led to the yard behind. Max and Ditta slowed and stopped their bikes. Peering in, they could make out a parking lot and loading bay and long sheds open at the front so the various sizes of timber could be inspected and admired.

Ditta and Max walked into the yard and leaned their bikes against a shed wall.

'The recycled timber's back there,' said Max. 'I know the way. Come on.'

He was so eager that just for a moment Ditta felt he was taking over. But she had to admit he did know more about the timber yard than her, so she followed him past the sheds and out into a wide space where drivers could turn their loaded trucks. Beyond this big open circle were even more sheds. A man in blue overalls watched them coming across the open space.

'Hi there, Max,' the man called.

'Hi, Tyke!' Max called back. 'It's Tyke Roberts,' he muttered sideways to Ditta. 'He's a sort of second cousin of mine.'

'So what can I do for you?' Tyke Roberts asked as they came up to him. 'Or is this just a friendly call?'

And now Max who, only a moment ago, had been leading the way, hesitated.

'Well . . .' he began, 'the thing is . . .'

Ditta took over. After all she was the great detective. Max was merely her helper. It was time she took charge again.

'We're doing a project at school,' she said quickly. 'A project on the timber industry. We have to do research on — on planting trees and cutting them down and sawing them up and all that. And Max said a lot of the wood used in his house was recycled and came from here, so we thought we'd check up on its history.'

A curious look crossed Tyke's face. For a moment he looked cautious . . . more than cautious. He looked apprehensive. All in a moment his face straightened itself again, but Ditta and Max had already seen a quick flicker of fear. Tyke began talking rapidly. Funnily enough, just for a moment he sounded rather like a member of the Old Baldy family.

'Wonderful wood, that! Wonderful! Well-weathered . . . mature . . . wood from native trees. You know we have some of the world's best timber here in New Zealand. Slow-growing, of course, and slow-growing's awkward for a booming timber industry. I mean if you really want to boom you need to have a bit of speed. That's why treated pine has taken off.'

'Recycled,' Ditta repeated in a firm voice, reminding him of what they really should be talking about. 'That means the wood was used in some other house before it was used in Max's, doesn't it?'

'Yeah!' said Tyke, and once again he looked unwilling to talk to them. He glanced at the timber racks behind him as if something stacked among the wooden timbers might be secretly listening. 'Look, this is my work time,' he said. 'I can't just stand around yakking to you kids.'

'No . . . hang about!' Ditta said quickly. 'This

won't take long. The wood that was used in Max's house . . . where did that come from?'

Tyke licked his lips nervously. 'Now you're asking!' he said. 'How would I know? Hey . . .would-wood! How wood I know!' He laughed loudly, then stopped laughing and looked at them reproachfully. 'It's a pun,' he said.

Ditta and Max stared back at him.

'You do know, don't you?' Ditta said. 'You know there was something funny about that wood. And we know you know. So tell us! Tell us about the wood that was used in Max's house.'

'It's not like a state secret, is it?' Max added.

Tyke shifted his weight from his right foot to his left then back again. 'Came from an old house . . . an old house over on Croyden's Hill, funnily enough, because Croyden's Hill was well out of town, back then. Just the one house on it — a big old place,' he went on, waving vaguely. 'No one had lived there for ages. Good wood in it though,' he added quickly.

'Which house?' asked Ditta. 'Whose house was it?

'It'd been rented out for years . . . well, actually it *had* been hard to rent,' said Tyke looking suspiciously vague. And then . . .'

'Didn't people call it a haunted house?' Ditta asked daringly. 'That's why it was hard to rent, wasn't it? I mean kids at school used to say it was haunted . . .' She was only guessing, but going halfway like this might encourage Tyke to finish things off by telling them anything else he had to tell.

'Only a few nutters ever said that! I mean who believes in ghosts?' said Tyke quickly. 'Take it from me, the wood in that house was spot-on . . . sound, mature wood. Criminal to waste it! And who believes in ghosts?' he repeated.

Ditta looked at him sternly. His eyes quickly twisted away.

'You do,' she said, and knew she was right. She rhymed at him. 'You were scared to let on that the wood might be haunted, in case any buyers grew nervous and daunted.'

Tyke rolled his eyes, tilted his head, took two steps north, and then shuffled half a step east. 'Great!' he said. 'Here I am, trying to get my work done, and Shakespeare's sister turns up, spouting poetry.'

'Tell us!' Max shouted, sounding desperate, and suddenly Tyke relaxed.

'OK! OK!' he cried. 'I can't tell you much, but I'll tell you what I know. I know the house was out there, falling to bits, with no one living in it. And I know my boss made the old man an offer for it. And . . .'

'Which old man?' asked Ditta, wondering how some old man had become part of the story.

'Old man Garibaldi!' said Tyke. 'You see him getting around — that old bloke who never stops talking about his laptop. He must be ninety if he's a day.'

'Old Baldy!' Ditta screamed.

'That's him!' said Tyke. 'White hair and beard.'

'I thought his first name was Garry,' said Max. 'I thought he was called Garry Baldy. Because I did feel it was a bit strange — him having a nickname like that when he was so hairy.'

'I felt it first,' cried Ditta, determined that nobody should know more about Old Baldy than she did.

'Well, you're almost right,' said Tyke. 'His name's all one word though — Garibaldi. It's an Italian name.'

'And he used to live in the house the haunted

timber was recycled from?' asked Max.

Tyke looked uncertain. 'I think he lived in it when he was a kid. But, like I said, that was ages ago — I mean you've only got to look at him to know that — and the house had been rented out and then rented out again. And then it was deserted. It was falling to bits when we made him an offer.'

'Right! Thanks!' said Ditta, trying to sound like an efficient detective once more. 'We'll check up with Mr Garibaldi for our next bit of research.'

'Better you than me,' said Tyke. 'If you write down half of what he has to tell you that project will fill ten books. And more, probably. Probably enough to fill a whole library — that old joker never stops talking. But I suppose when you're ninety you've got a lot left over you want to tell people about.'

'I'll bet Old Baldy doesn't know much about computers,' said Max a little later, muttering as they pulled their bikes out of the bike stand.

'Well, he thinks he does. Remember he carries his laptop around with him,' Ditta pointed out. 'But he might know even more about ghosts and haunted, recycled floor boards, which is what we need to be told about right now. Number one . . . no, hang on! That was Hilly, and I've sort of solved Hilly. I'm carrying him around in my school pack. So Old Baldy can be number one now, and you can keep on being number two because you're not quite solved yet, Max. And Mirabel's still number three. So! Number four — ghost data!

CHAPTER 10

THEY had raced though town after school anxious to get to Woodcraft Timber Supplies. Now they biked back again rather more slowly, taking it in turns to lead, and shouting backwards and forwards to one another.

'Old Baldy might remember something,' yelled Ditta back over her shoulder. 'Mind you, old people can be really forgetful.'

'He could forget everything else in the world but he wouldn't forget that ghost,' shouted Max, and his bike wobbled as if simply remembering the ghost made him unreliable on the road.

'Well, I reckon Old Baldy remembers every single thing that's ever happened to him since he was born,' Ditta added, mainly to herself.

The park came into sight again . . . the big trees, the distant cricket ground . . . and there, right in front of them, the little lake. There were the ducks and there was old Baldy . . . Mr Garibaldi . . . staring at the water as if he were enjoying the reflections. His laptop sat on his knee like a patient and slightly neglected pet.

Ditta and Max stopped a little distance away from him and propped their bikes against one of the trees. Ditta peered into her backpack and spoke to the blue book nestling quietly among her papers and project-notes.

'Don't you go suddenly appearing,' she said, her voice soft but stern. 'He's an old man and a sudden ghost might scare him to death.' The book didn't stir. It was hard to be sure if Hilly could hear anything she was saying. But then a ghostly whisper came hissing up out of her pack. 'I'll just listen in,' said the whisper. 'Anyhow, I don't like bright light.' So Ditta hooked her pack over one shoulder, straightened herself a little, and she and Max closed in on Old Baldy, moving quietly . . . rather shyly. All the same he must have heard something. He looked up quickly.

'Nice day!' said Ditta, which wasn't much of a beginning but it was better than nothing.

'Nice day . . .' Old Baldy cried, as if he'd just thought of this himself and was telling them something they didn't already know. 'And by now a man like me (what with remembering a lot of nice days) feels like a real judge of them, so I was just sitting here, trying to work out if the nice days now are as nice as nice days used to be when I was your age, only I can't make up my mind, which you'd think I *would* be able to, because, not having to work, I do have time to think things through, since, when you've got the space just to sit around and look at the water, you've got plenty of thinking time, which is why I try to feed my impressions into this machine here on my knee from time to time, yet on the other hand . . .'

'Are you really Mr Garibaldi?' asked Ditta, though she already knew he was. Still when you're determined to cut your way through a tangle of serpent sentences you have to begin somewhere. Old Baldy paused and looked uncertain, though not for long. He puffed to himself, then off he went again.

'Mr Garibaldi?' he said. 'I used to be him, so I suppose I still am, seeing it's the name I was born to and then registered by, and when they send me those government forms and so on, not to mention my pension (which I'm more than entitled to, being over ninety as I already told you) they call me Mr Garibaldi, very respectful and respectable and so on, but it's ages since anyone actually called me by my real name since Old Baldy is what people mostly call me now . . . though mind you I've got more hair than a lot of the ones who call me bald, so it makes me laugh, but then a good laugh always does you good I say, so . . .'

'We're doing historical research,' Ditta said firmly. 'We wanted to ask you about something.'

'. . . and when it comes to asking about history, you've come to the right person,' cried Old Baldy warmly, just as if he'd been planning to say this from the very beginning, 'because I'm someone who can tell anybody anything about anything historical, seeing that, though I'm old, my memory keeps on going and I've got more tucked away in it than a lot of people twice my age, not that there is anyone twice my age, because if they were twice my age they'd be a hundred and eighty, and as far as I know there hasn't been anyone who . . .'

'It's about a house you used to live in ages ago,' said Ditta. 'Back when you were a kid. Your family owned it. It was a house up on Croyden Hill and . . .'

And here she stopped. Old Baldy had started back, stiffened up and twisted around to stare at them from under his bushy white eyebrows. His little black eyes seemed to sink back into his head as they were suddenly afraid of what she might be about to show him.

'A man like me has lived in a good few houses over the years,' he said in a soft crinkling voice and then fell silent, which was so unexpected that for a moment neither Max nor Ditta quite believed in the silence. But then both Ditta and Max began talking flat out, one after the other, trying to get in as much as they could before Old Baldy started up again.

'This was back when you were a boy,' Ditta said, reminding him even though she was sure he remembered.

'They pulled the house down — the house you used to live in — about a year ago,' cried Max.

'The wood was recycled,' Ditta added.

'My bedroom floor is made from wood from your old house,' Max explained, interrupting her. 'And at night it moans and twists around. The wood's got a voice, and it speaks. I know it's trying to tell me something but I can't make out the words.'

'Was your house haunted when you lived in it?' asked Ditta.

'How did it come to be haunted?' asked Max. 'Do you know what it's trying to say?'

Old Baldy threw up his hands, like a soldier surrendering and anxious to show he has no weapons.

'Stop! Stop!' he shouted. 'Too many questions! Too many!'

'Only one question,' said Ditta. 'Was your old house haunted?'

'Yes!' said Baldy. 'Not that everyone could see the ghost. Not everyone could hear it either. But I could. When I was a child I told them. I told them over and over again, then over again one more time, but no one believed me.'

There was another silence.

'I believe you,' Max said at last, 'because whatever-it-is is haunting me too. And no one believes me either. Well, no one but Ditta.'

The old man buried his face in his hands, sighing through his fingers in a way that made his beard ripple. He began one of his endless sentences but whispering by now so the words were muffled by his white whiskers. Ditta leaned closer, listening hard.

'Isn't there any end to it?' he was muttering. 'So angry . . . so angry . . . such ancient anger going on and on and on, even if everything it has to be angry about is all in the past . . .'

Ditta was suddenly frightened that Hilly might decide to put in his own ghostly oar. Somehow she felt sure it wasn't a good thing for Old Baldy to be distracted by an actual ghost at this moment. Let him get used to the idea that other people knew about his family haunting before bringing him face to face with an actual ghost. But Hilly chose to stay haunting the book in her pack, though no doubt he was listening.

'I have a story to tell,' Old Baldy said. 'But no interrupting me. I can't stand interruption.'

Then he began to tell his story.

CHAPTER 11

I᷈ᴛ goes a long way back,' Old Baldy began. 'Two hundred years, which is a long time, even to me and I've been getting around for half that time . . . no, I tell a lie . . . for almost half of it . . .' He was quickly getting over his moment of horror and beginning to enjoy the chance to talk without interruption. Max gave Ditta a despairing glance. This story might easily take the rest of the day . . . and most of the night as well.

'. . . for almost half of it,' Old Baldy was repeating. 'It began back in 1803, give or take a year, that is, because I'm only telling you what was told to me, and I don't know exactly what year it was and I don't think anyone else knows exactly, because nobody wrote it down back then, bearing in mind that there weren't quite so many people who could write back then as nowadays, let alone anyone wanting to be exact . . . but, anyway, I digress, being able to comment on the state of affairs in the past more than most people can, so I do whenever I get the chance.

'So anyhow, there was this ship, back then, anchored off the coast out there — did I mention that Croyden was the captain's name? They named that hill after him . . . you know the one I mean . . . they've just subdivided it. But anyway back then it seems this party of men came ashore . . . up the beach . . . which wasn't the beach as we know it now . . . but up they came, and probably right through here whcre this park is now. They were just ordinary seamen, but the ship's bosun, he came with them, just to keep them in order and make sure they didn't desert the ship by running off into the back country maybe . . . it was a tough life at sea in those days you know, not like now . . .'

'Did they get as far as the hills?' asked Ditta, trying to hurry him along.

'I'm coming to that,' said Baldy. 'Don't worry-hurry me, just let the story flow along out of me, because, anyhow, as I was saying before you interrupted me, they came up here . . . the ship being anchored out there.' He waved his hand in the direction of the sea, which couldn't be seen from the park. All the same, as he waved his hand Ditta heard the waves, faint and far beyond the town, sighing their eternal sigh on the unseen sand.

'The trees came right down to the water in those days, it was all forest . . .' As he spoke, Baldy stretched his arms high then wide, sketching the shape of that vanished forest and the beach where those men had once landed.

'Anyhow they were gone a long time and then they came back — the able seamen . . . the sailors, that is . . . and told Captain Croyden the bosun had an accident, falling onto rocks. And to cut a long story short they declared he'd killed himself and was dead as a door nail, and you can't get much more dead than a door nail . . . unless it's a coffin nail, ha, ha, ha! Did I mention him being a bosun? Well, I think he was, but I don't totally remember, being only a little kid when that story was first told to me, though, mind you, it only seems like yesterday, my having this good memory which I may have mentioned to you. But anyway he was dead, dead as a door nail or coffin nail, no doubt about it, so Captain Croyden gave orders and they buried him and dug up this little seedling tree and planted it on his grave just to give him a bit of recognition, as it were. A matai tree it must have been — or that's what I think now — and then they all got back on their ship and sailed away . . . sadder and wiser men, no doubt. Now the thing is (and this will surprise you), one of those men was my great-grandfather and that's how I know this story because he told my grandfather and my grandfather told my father and he told me and now I'm telling you, and so the story flows on . . . the way they do. Now, here I skip fifty years . . . sixty maybe . . .'

'Thank goodness,' muttered Max. Yet for all that he was listening closely.

'. . . and back we come to this part of the world, not my great-grandfather, that first one I mentioned, but his son, my grandfather, bringing a wife and kids with him. The

Garibaldis — did I mention he was a Garibaldi like me?'

'No,' said Ditta 'but I sort of guessed.'

'Well, he was a Garibaldi,' said Baldy. 'It began as an Italian name, well-respected in that part of the world. But I'll tell you all about that later. He arrived back here, my grandfather did . . . arrived with his family. But by then it was all different, of course, because they'd cleared the land by then . . . not those sailors I mentioned, but a later lot . . . settlers we call them because they came here to settle . . . and they needed to make room for houses and farms. Anyhow, he looked around, my grandfather did, and bought his bit of land . . . that very land with the hill on it where the bosun had been buried, and which my grandfather knew something about because he'd been told the story over and over again, the same story I've just told you.

'And he farmed a bit, my granddad. It was hard, but him and his lot made it, one way and another. And he cleared the bush the way they did in those days . . . but he never cut the tree that grew where his father's old friend had been buried.

'It had grown by then, of course, the way

trees do, but he'd worked out which one it must have been, since it was set a bit apart from all the rest, and anyway he had a feeling about it, which he'd probably inherited. They say he — well, the family story is — that he kept clear of the tree . . . was shy of it . . . respected it in some way. Are you with me so far?'

'Yes,' said Ditta and Max together.

'Well then,' said the old man, 'things being the way they are — the way they were, that is to say — everything went well for our lot, and the word 'lot' is what they call the operative word, because there did come to be quite a lot of us, and the first house became too small for a family of sixteen, the way houses can do, if you know what I mean.'

'Yes we know,' said Ditta and Max, both sighing. Max sighed because the new room, the room that was to have been all his own, had turned out to be so impossible, and Ditta sighed too, thinking how hard it was to get near the computer with a nerd of a sister crouching over it day and night.

'So, suddenly, back then, there were plans to build a bigger house . . . just plans. And my father . . . it was my father by then, for my grandfather was too old to think straight (though he wasn't as old as me and I can still think straight enough, so I must take after my grandmother's side of the family) . . . anyhow, my father was the one to do the family thinking at that time, and he decided we'd be needing a new house somewhere down the line and . . . well, he had no reason to think twice about the tree on the hillside.

'He had it cut down and turned into timber. Not that we used it straight off. It was left to weather first, because that's what you do with timber. But also, about that time there were family complications, what with the war beginning soon after — not the Hitler war but the one before that . . .'

'The First World War . . .' put in Ditta, because sitting quietly and saying nothing for a long time just wasn't natural.

'Right! That's the very one!' said Baldy. 'I don't remember the first bit, being born towards the end of it but . . .'

'When did your father actually build the house?' asked Ditta, interrupting him again. Old Baldy gave her a reproachful look, but he did begin to hurry his long story just a little.

'That wasn't until after the war,' he said. 'Of course there was all sorts of timber used in the house, and a bit of quarry stone from down the road . . . but one sure thing is that timber from the old tree was used, and that's where the troubles began . . . because me and my brother, we had a room built with some of that wood, and right off we had trouble.'

'Did the floor seethe at night?' Max asked.

'Not the floor, the walls,' said Old Baldy. 'That wood had been used in the walls and — yes — it did seethe, and it kept on complaining. *I'm so lonely!* it said, and kept on saying it, over and over. *Left behind and lonely!* it kept saying, all night, being really sorry for itself, and that wasn't the only thing it said.

'Over and over again it said . . .' Old Baldy stopped, stared into space, then blinked a few times. 'Well never mind that! The thing was we couldn't sleep, my brother and I, and the other thing was that no one believed us for a while.'

'Did it moan?' asked Max.

'Moan? You bet it moaned. Moan! Moan! Moan! It went on and on, being really sorry for itself, and, like I said, we couldn't sleep, though we could talk back to it, not that we had much to say, being too terrified. And my dad — my old dad — he wasn't like dads nowadays, helping with the dishes and all that. Mind you, he did have this herd of cows to watch over, and back then a farmer had to milk all his cows by hand, twice a day, too, morning and night— '

'Forget the milking. Just tell us what your dad said,' asked Ditta sternly. 'About the moaning walls.'

'He said we didn't work hard enough,' said Old Baldy. 'He said that if we worked harder we'd be so tired we'd sleep even if the walls screamed at us. Fact was he didn't and wouldn't believe us, but our mother did, because — see — we were so wakeful and frightened it was making us ill . . . me and my brother, that is . . . and being a good mother she knew something was up.

'And then, at last, something else must have happened. I was never clear what it was, back then, because it wasn't talked about, not really, only in whispers with people shutting up and rolling their eyes if their little ones came into the room.

'But whatever it was, my dad came over very thoughtful and one day he announced we were going to sell the house. I heard them talking about it . . . my mother and father. *Why don't you pull the wood from that old tree out of the walls? I heard my mother saying. Pull it out, burn it and replace it.* But my father said the house was worth a lot as it stood, and would sell like a hot cake, with the town creeping out towards us. So, first off, we subdivided the farm like they're subdividing all Croyden Hill these days . . . sold the cows, too . . . that was sad . . . I liked those cows . . . liked the milk all frothy and warm straight from the cow . . .'

'Did you sell the house?' asked Ditta.

'Well, we didn't wait for that,' said Old Baldy. 'We had the chance of a new place down by the beach, so we moved out quickly, renting the old place to go on with. So we suddenly started living out there on the edge of town.

'Not that it was *town* in the way it is now, but the whole place was stretching out and so were we. And I . . .'

'What about the people who rented your house?' asked Max.

'That's just it,' cried Old Baldy triumphantly. 'They moved on within the year. And the next lot. Then it stood empty for a while, with no one wanting to buy it, and then someone took out a lease on it. Now that lot — they were determined, and when they had a bit of the old seething-and-moaning trouble they had engineers in to inspect the walls and the foundations and work out just what was going on with the house, but in the end it was too much for them.

'Up went the notice at the gate . . . For Sale or Rent . . . and about then I got work in another town and lost touch with it all one way and another . . . my brother might be able to tell you. Oh no, hang about! He's dead, isn't he?'

'Did people ever say your house was haunted?' asked Max.

'Say it? Of course they said it. Over and over again they said it. Over and over! Said it secretly for the most part, because no one wants to let on they really believe in ghosts . . . well, only a few loonies . . . and . . .'

'So after a while no one wanted to buy the house,' said Max. 'Or rent it.'

'That's right,' agreed Old Baldy. 'Word had got around there was something wrong with it. Some said ghosts and some said drains, but either way it stood around, and stood around, and after a while it was as if people had forgotten it was there. Or just didn't want to talk about it, most likely . . .'

'. . . and in the end the house got pulled down,' Ditta put in firmly. 'But its timber was still good, so it was recycled.'

'And my dad bought the timber and used it in our house,' said Max.

Old Baldy had certainly been talking to them, but in a funny way he'd been talking to himself too, staring up and out as if he were watching some soap opera on an invisible television set high in the air.

Now he looked at Max as if he were really seeing him for the first time.

'The wood from that old house?' he said at last, '. . . the old house that used to be my house when I was little . . . you say that wood has been built into your house? Is that what you're pestering me to know about?'

'That's right,' said Max. 'The floor in my room is made from wood left over from your old house.'

'You've got trouble then. By jingo, have you got trouble!' said Old Baldy, and leaning back in the seat he fell silent at last, folding his hands over his laptop computer as if he were comforting a pet, and staring out at the ducks, obviously glad the trouble had passed on and now belonged to someone else.

CHAPTER 12

'RIGHT!' said Ditta sitting at the desk in her room and setting out pages in front of her. The blue book sat beside her pages and Hilly sat on the edge of her desk, none the worse for the sunlight but looking clearer and brighter in the shadows. 'I think I've got things in some sort of order.'

She cleared her throat.

'Number one. Back in history a ship landed in the bay and one of the men had a fall and was killed. They buried him up on the hill and planted a tree over him. Number two. A hundred years later that tree was cut down and turned into timber and then after a while — number three — Old Baldy's family built a house out of it. But right from the beginning the house was haunted. Not everyone saw the ghost but a lot of people did . . . well, they saw the floor seething and they heard the boards complaining. Old Baldy did.'

'Maybe not a ghost. Maybe just a ghost effect,' Max said, not wanting Ditta to be in total command of his ghost. 'The floor moaned and . . .'

'It was a ghost,' said Hilly. 'It still is.'

'I'm counting it as a ghost,' said Ditta, sweeping on grandly. 'Anyhow the Garibaldis did their best to stay on, but the haunting was too much for them and so they moved out . . .'

'. . . and tried to sell their house,' Max said, taking over firmly. 'But whoever lived in the house after that didn't stay there long . . . and then, after a while no one wanted to rent it.'

'So the house was pulled down . . .' Hilly said.

'And we bought the recycled wood,' groaned Max, 'and we used it to . . .'

'. . . you used it for the floor in your house,'

Ditta cut in, 'and the ghost came along with it so now your bedroom is haunted.'

'And my computer!' groaned Max.

'That's right,' said Ditta, shuddering in spite of herself as she remembered that swirling throat and snarling mouth, breathing hatred and despair into the world. 'You've not only got a haunted floor but a haunted computer. Weird!'

'A haunted computer?' said a voice behind them. Ditta spun around. There was her little sister, leaning in the doorway, listening. Ditta could tell at a glance that the mention of haunted computers had caught Mirabel's interest.

'We were talking about ghosts,' she said quickly. 'This is my room and we're talking private stuff. Get out!' From the corner of her eye she could see Hilly tactfully sliding back towards the book.

'You were talking about a computer,' said Mirabel, 'and I know more about computers than you do.'

'We were talking about ghosts!' declared Ditta. 'And you're not interested in ghosts. Get out.'

'I'm sort of interested in ghosts,' said Mirabel.

'If Max Bryant has got a haunted computer you should ask me about it. And there's no need for that library ghost to try hiding himself. I'm used to seeing him by now.'

'Mind your own business . . .' Ditta began. But then she stopped and looked over at Max. 'She really does know a lot about computers,' she said. 'And she's already seen Hilly sitting in the library. Not everyone sees him. Shall we tell her?'

Max groaned.

'I suppose so,' he said. 'And then she'll tell all her friends. And soon the whole school will know I believe in ghosts.'

'I won't tell anyone,' said Mirabel. 'I'm very silent.'

'Except at home,' said Ditta.

'Home's different,' said Mirabel. 'I'm allowed to argue about things at home. That's what home's there for . . . for arguing about things.'

As they talked, Ditta was looking at Mirabel and thinking hard. A successful detective knows how to make use of other people's powers.

'She really is good with computers,' she said to Max.

'So am I!' cried Max, insulted at the

suggestion that a girl of nine might have more computer power than him.

'No, hang on!' Ditta said. 'She's more than good with them. She's really good . . . better than Dad. Better than me,' she admitted unwillingly. 'She can work them with her eyes shut.'

Max didn't exactly back off. Even when he was being haunted he wasn't a backing-off sort of boy. He slid sideways.

'So do you reckon she might be able to put up with that ghost roaring out of the computer?' he asked.

'Maybe not,' said Ditta. 'But we could try. We've got to try something. We don't quite know the what or why, but, anyway, we have to try.'

CHAPTER 13

ONCE again they were at Max's house. Max's mother hugged him while Max looked sideways to see if Ditta was laughing at a boy of his age being hugged. But Ditta was nodding as if she understood, while Mirabel stared vaguely into space as she so often did.

'I've missed you,' said Max's mother. 'The house felt sort of strange without you . . . well, your bedroom did, in a funny, echoing way.'

'That's because it's haunted,' said Max. 'I keep telling you.'

'You and your ghosts,' said his mother,

but, although her words were the sort of words a mother uses when her children talk about ghosts, her voice was somehow more doubtful . . . more uncertain . . . than it had been yesterday.

'Mind you, I do understand why you might imagine there are a few ghosts around. You see last night I dreamed . . . no, I didn't exactly dream . . . I heard . . . that is I . . .' she stopped. 'Oh nothing!' she said quickly. 'What are you kids going to do?'

'We're going to check the ghost out,' said Ditta. 'We're on its trail so it had better watch out.'

Max's mother's face cleared. She laughed like a normal mother. 'Oh well! Go to it!' she said, sounding this time as if she thought they were playing a game, and she was playing along with them. 'Good luck!'

All the same Ditta couldn't help shuddering in a secret, inside way as they crowded into Max's room once more, although his neatly made bed looked like an ordinary bed and his chair, half-turned from his desk, spread its arms wide in a welcoming way.

Everything seemed tidy and almost ordinary,

yet Ditta thought she knew why Max's mother had been looking rather more uncertain than she had yesterday. In spite of the neatness there was a clammy feeling in the air and, though the screen of the computer was as ordinary and square as the screen of any computer, Ditta knew for sure there was something nameless lurking on its other side . . . lurking there and looking out at her.

'There it is,' Max began, talking to Mirabel. 'You touch that button there.' But Mirabel was already marching up to the computer, smiling as she sat down in front of it as if she and the computer were already old friends. She peered into its screen rather like a doctor peering into the eyes of a patient in need of comfort and cure.

There was a disk sitting on the bench beside the computer.

'What's on this?' Mirabel asked, pointing at it. 'Anything that matters?'

'Music,' said Max. 'That guy with the purple hair — Battering Bob Bashful.'

But Mirabel was already slipping the disk into a slip in front of Max's computer, just as if the computer was hers and she had been using it for years. *Easy Front Access,* said words on the front of the computer. Mirabel certainly made the access look particularly easy.

She turned the computer on. It hummed to itself. And then the screen exploded outward with that evil green light and the computer roared at Mirabel, sounding almost like a lion but nastier than any lion . . . almost like the sea but more savage than the sea. For though the sea can sound furious with the land and sky, it never quite sounds as if it hates itself and wants to tear itself to pieces.

Mirabel swayed back from the screen. Her hair lifted and swirled and tangled as if a wind were blowing out of the screen at her, though there was no wind, just that terrible snarling. Her face turned green, reflecting the green light which seemed to be flowing, not from a screen but up through some throat and out through a square mouth, hungry enough to tear the world to bits.

This time, thought Ditta, *there really did seem to be words tossing around in all that anger* and, though she really didn't want to hear what those words might be, her ears still strained, trying to work them out. It was alarming to find her own ears were rebelling against her and making up their own minds about when they wanted to hear.

'They . . .' the voice was saying. 'They . . . they killed . . . they killed . . . they killed me.'

Mirabel stared at the screen, then took a deep breath. Anyone could tell she was working herself up to do something scary.

'Mirabel!' Ditta shouted, suddenly frightened in a new way. A sister can be really irritating at times, but, all the same, Ditta didn't want her to come to any harm. 'Mirabel! Don't!'

But Mirabel, holding her left forearm half across her eyes, bent towards the computer. She put her hand over the mouse, then squeaked and let it go.

Ditta knew just how that mouse must have felt, throbbing like a pulpy heart, under Mirabel's palm. 'Mirabel! Watch out!' she called.

But Mirabel closed her eyes and bent even close to the screen. She clapped her hand firmly over the mouse once more and shifted it sideways. A spark of fire shot from one side of the computer screen-mouth to the other. Mirabel seemed like a magical dentist drilling at unseen teeth of an invisible monster. Her right forefinger clicked down on the mouse.

She slid the mouse over the mouse pad, then, once again, Ditta saw that right forefinger dancing. The computer mouth howled out at them . . .

. . . and then, suddenly it fell silent. The oozing green was gone. All gone! The usual computer screen drifted back towards them, pale and blank and still. Mirabel quickly pushed a button. Her fingers danced on the keyboard for a third time, then dropped away.

'What are you doing?' Ditta cried.

Mirabel pressed down on the left side of the mouse.

'Where's it gone?' Max was asking.

Mirabel blinked, touching the front of the computer rather as if she were comforting it before she turned to look at them. Her freckles stood out as if they had just been painted on. Ditta realised that, though Mirabel had seemed so cool and capable, she had actually turned pale. There was no doubt about it. She had been very frightened.

'I didn't know if it would work,' Mirabel said. 'But I think it has. I thought it was worth a go.'

'What did you do?' Max asked again.

'I saved the ghost onto that disk,' she said. 'It's probably wiped your Battering Bob music, but at least you should be able to use the computer again.' She pressed another button on the front of the computer, and the disk shot out into the world once more, rather as if the computer were poking a square black tongue out at them.

Mirabel flicked the disk out and stood there, holding it gingerly. 'Quick! We'd better find somewhere safe to put it. Most programs would stay put, but a ghost — well, a ghost might work out a way to get free from a disk.'

CHAPTER 14

MAX and Ditta both stared at the disk. Then they looked up, staring at Mirabel. Then they stared down at the disk again. Neither of them had ever worked out that a ghost might be saved to disk. Then Max slammed his right fist in the palm of his left hand.

'Yes!' he shouted, making his *yes* mean *Hooray!* and *Thank you!* and a lot of other powerful, happy things all mixed up together.

'Didn't you . . .' Ditta began, looking at Mirabel curiously, 'Weren't you terrified by that mouth? That green throat?'

Mirabel puffed out her cheeks.

'I was scared, but the screen sort of breathed out at me and made my glasses go all foggy,' she said. 'I knew something was there, but I couldn't see it very well so perhaps that sort of saved me. And I thought I'd just try . . .'

'But how could you see what to press or where to point the cursor to save anything on any disk?' Max asked, and Mirabel laughed.

'I can work computers with my eyes shut,' she said. 'Even if I couldn't see the toolbar I'd still know where it was . . . and I know the tool bar by heart. You press *File* and then you go to *Save as* and then at the top there's a little panel which . . .'

'OK! OK!' said Ditta just a little impatiently, because no one wants a smaller sister to be too clever. 'Do you think that horrible, green, slimy ghost, or whatever it is, is really on that disk? I mean it might still be in the floorboards . . .'

But looking at the floor she had the strangest feeling that something in the room had certainly changed . . . somehow there was a difference in the air around her.

She was as sure as she could be that the room was no longer haunted.

'What we must do now,' Max was declaring, 'is to drive a stake through the heart of that disk. That's the way you get rid of vampires. Let's do it now, before the ghost works out a way of getting free.'

'I don't think the ghost was a vampire,' said Ditta. 'What we should do next is find a box made of something ghosts can't go through and lock the ghost in it. Can they go through silver?'

'I don't know. And anyway where would we get a silver box?' asked Mirabel.

'We should just put a stake through it,' said Max.

'No,' said another voice and there, standing among them, was Hilly, wavering like a boy painted on the air . . . then growing stronger and more sure of himself. 'I've been waiting around, silent for ages,' he said. 'But now it's time you listened to me.'

Mirabel let out a small squawk.

'It's that library ghost,' she cried. 'How did he get here?'

'He doesn't haunt the library,' said Ditta. 'He haunts a book, and the book is in my school bag. He's a portable ghost.' She had forgotten she was carrying Hilly around with her.

And suddenly she felt as if she was the one person in the room who understood everything that was going on . . . she was in charge again. 'Hilly's our expert on ghosts. I mean — being a ghost himself he knows about other ghosts. So — OK, Hilly — how do we get rid of this ghost now that it's portable too?'

'We exercise it,' said Mirabel. 'That's what you do with ghosts. You exercise them.'

'Not *exercise* . . . it's *exorcise*!' cried Ditta, suddenly remembering the right word. 'Hilly, we don't mind you. You're great. But this ghost is horrible. How do we exorcise this horrible ghost?'

'It is horrible,' Hilly agreed, 'but it's horrible because it's so unhappy. Something happened to it back . . . you know . . . back in the past and it can't rest. I mean I can't rest because I never finished that book of mine. And I don't mind not resting because I'm one of those ghosts who are still interested in things.

'This ghost needs to tell its story, and I think that's what it's been trying to do. But it doesn't know how to do its telling, and for a long time nobody has been able hear it. Even when they *could* hear it, nobody has wanted to listen. Not being listened to makes a ghost angry and this one has got angrier and angrier for over a hundred years. That's a lot of saved-up anger.'

'Don't try understanding it!' cried Max. 'It's a horror. And anyhow we can't understand it. It talks a ghost language all its own.'

'But I might be able to understand it,' said Hilly. 'I'm a bit scared of it too, but I don't mind trying.'

'But how do we — how do we set up a meeting?' asked Mirabel. 'It's there on the disk and we don't want it to get back into the computer again, or into the floorboards either. That ghost's over here on disk and you're over there, haunting your book . . .'

'I know a bit about computers from watching you play with them in the school library,' said Hilly. 'I can't tell for sure, but I think if you put the book by the computer I might be able to slide into it somehow and find my way around . . . and then if you put the disk back into the computer . . .'

'Oh no! No way!' cried Max. 'That horrible ghost would just dart back through the wiring, swirl through the wall plug and back into the floorboards again.'

This seemed quite possible.

'The best way to close a ghost down is to complete it. And the best way to complete it . . .' — Hilly hesitated — '. . . is to let it tell its story. Stories are important to ghosts. Telling our stories sets us free.'

'I'm not having it back in my computer,' said Max obstinately.

'But . . .' said Hilly, 'maybe another sort of computer might do. Do all computers plug into the wall?'

Ditta and Max looked at one another. Max's face began to change and lighten.

'There are laptops . . .' began Mirabel.

'Hey,' began Max. 'I . . .'

'Hey!' cried Ditta triumphantly, getting in ahead of Max. 'I know!'

And she felt she did know. She was the one who would be able to solve all their problems. It was a wonderful feeling.

'Old Baldy's laptop!' she explained to Mirabel. 'He carries it about with him, showing it off. And he knows about the history of this ghost.'

'He won't want it in his floorboards though,' said Max.

'No,' agreed Ditta, 'but listen! Listen!' She

took a breath and looked around. Everyone was listening. Great! 'Number one,' she proclaimed, holding up one finger. 'Old Baldy will be home by now, so we take the disk to his house and explain things. Number two! We put Hilly's book beside Baldy's laptop, so that, maybe, Hilly can get into the laptop . . .'

'. . . if I can,' said Hilly. 'I'm not sure if I will be able to, but I feel so sorry for that ghost I don't mind trying.'

'. . . and then, number three, we put the disk in and . . . and see what happens.'

'I saved the ghost under 'GHOST',' said Mirabel. 'So if we put the disk in . . . if it works we ought to be able to pull the ghost back up onto the screen again. But it might be dangerous. I mean when I saved it a few minutes ago I took it by surprise. Next time it might be prepared.'

'Or we might save Hilly to the disk along with the ghost,' said Max. 'They might get mixed into each other.'

'We can't tell what will happen,' said Ditta firmly. 'But let's try. Let's do things in order. Number one!' she cried. 'Before we try any of this let's make sure that Hilly can get into computers.' She dragged the blue book out of her pack and slammed the book down beside the computer. 'Go to it, Hilly.'

'I'll try!' said Hilly and disappeared, which made Mirabel squeak again, then look at them apologetically.

'I'm used to seeing him sitting in the library, not just appearing and disappearing,' she explained. She turned to Max. 'Shall I turn your computer on again? I mean the disk isn't in it, so it should be safe . . .'

'Give it a go,' said Max rather crossly, 'though I still feel we should drive a stake through the heart of that disk, just to be on the safe side.'

But Mirabel had already turned the computer on. Anyone could tell she had been planning to turn it on anyway, and had only pretended to consult Max out of politeness.

'Hey! Wow! Look at that!' cried Max, pointing. The screen of his computer glowed as if the sun was rising somewhere behind it, then burst into wonderful colour. And there was Hilly looking back at them from the screen, waving and smiling. His voice came to them, out of the speakers which stuck out like long, grey ears on either side of the screen.

'Can you see me?' Hilly was asking. 'I can see you.'

'You look great!' said Ditta. 'You're in full colour. And we can hear you. Can you hear us?'

'I can,' said Hilly. 'I don't quite know how, but I can.'

Ditta quickly took charge.

'OK!' she said. 'We know you can get into the computer and find your way around it. Next thing! Can you get out or do we have to save you to disk too?'

The screen went dark. A moment later Hilly stood among them once more, wavering once more, but grinning triumphantly.

'So far so good!' he cried. 'I can come and go. So let's find Old Baldy and ask him if we can use his laptop. You feed the disk in and bring the ghost up on the screen and I'll melt into the computer, and try to reason with it.'

'Right!' said Ditta. 'We've got a plan. Cool!' She looked at her watch. 'Let's go.'

'And let's get some fish and chips on the way,' said Max. 'I haven't wanted to eat much lately — but now, all of a sudden, I feel really hungry.'

CHAPTER 15

THEY went back through the park but the seat by the duck pond was empty. On through the park. Down Cinnamon Road. In at the green gate. They walked through the garden (Ditta leading the way), towards Old Baldy's door, which opened just before they got close enough to knock.

Old Baldy himself stood before them. They could tell at a glance he'd just arrived home from his usual duck feeding, and was still wearing his sheepskin jacket. It was hard to tell where his beard left off and his jacket began.

'Well now,' he said, looking delighted, but rather astonished at finding his doorstep crowded with visitors. 'Good day to you all . . . and it is a good day, isn't it, a good day for going for a walk or having people call in, always supposing they do happen to call in, which they don't very often nowadays, though, mind you, a few years ago it was all visitors, visitors, visitors, and I couldn't get rid of them back then, mostly likely because those were the days when I made my own cider, having too many apples in the autumn and needing to use them up somehow, but nowadays . . .'

'Grandpa!' called a voice from somewhere beyond him. 'Grandpa Garibaldi! You stop talking to yourself like that, because if the next-doors hear you (which they might, because, though they're not smart they're a nosy lot, and won't think twice about listening in to a babbling senior citizen) they'll think you're crazy, which you are, but we don't want them catching on . . .' Mrs Marrell's stream of words wound past them and out into the garden.

Old Baldy leaned forward.

'Listen to her — my granddaughter Maria,' he whispered in a hoarse voice. 'She's very kind-hearted but she never stops talking and once she begins she goes on forever.'

Mrs Marrell's background voice was still talking, telling Old Baldy what to do. Her long sentences were twining in and out of Old Baldy's own long sentences.

'. . . but she does tie my shoelaces for me,' he was saying, 'which is hard for me to do myself — not because of the knots, I can manage the knots — but because my back creaks when I bend over, and what with my back creaking and carrying on the way it does . . .'

'Sorry to interrupt you,' said Ditta firmly (not looking in the least bit sorry), 'but we've come to see you about that ghost we were discussing the other day. You know the one.'

Old Baldy fell sharply silent. There was nothing like the mention of the ghost to shut him up. He straightened; he pulled his wide mouth in tightly, and stared at them over his glasses, which were tilted crookedly across his nose.

'. . . and another thing,' his granddaughter was saying in the house behind him, 'while we're talking about the neighbours . . .'

'You've got a laptop computer and we wanted

to show you something on it,' Max said quickly, not wanting to get caught up in conversation about Old Baldy's neighbours. 'Mirabel here is a real expert so you don't have to worry that we'll crash it or anything.'

'What program do you run?' asked Mirabel.

Old Baldy's granddaughter came into the hall and peered past him at the children on the step. She had a red scarf tied around her hair and, after the first surprise, she seemed just as delighted to see them as Old Baldy had been.

'Visitors!' she cried. 'Oh, it's a long time since we had anyone drop in. How about a cup of tea and maybe a cake or two as well, if you like cake that is, which we all do, don't we, because there's nothing like cake, so don't let him keep you out there standing on the doorstep as if you were trying to sell him life insurance, not that there's any point in trying to sell life insurance to a man who's over ninety but you never know what people will try, and as for the money you have to pay for insurance when you get on a bit . . . well, it's a scandal, that's what I feel . . .'

Old Baldy spun around.

'They're friends of mine from the park,' he said. 'We meet there every now and then to

145

natter a bit where there aren't any interruptions such as a man can sometimes get at home, when he has the bad luck to live with someone who never stops talking. And they've called in so I can show them something on my computer, being only kids and not knowing much about technology, and me having that laptop I can play games on . . .'

But Mrs Marrell interrupted him. 'Ten to one they know twice as much as you,' she cried, 'because what you've got that laptop for I can't work out, since you never use it in any proper way, just sit there looking at the screen and tapping away and then complaining because it doesn't do what you think it ought to be doing, so . . .'

But Old Baldy shrugged his shoulders at her, turning to the children on the step in his own determined way.

'You come on in,' he said 'and I'll see if I can't help you with your problems, likewise you might be able to give me a bit of catch-up information about you-know-what, because you've been doing research, haven't you, and though it doesn't bother me any more (being all in the past as it were) I can't help being curious about it, what with it being one of the big things back in my remembering. And maybe she's right . . . this one here that keeps on interrupting us . . . a bit of cake might not be a bad idea because she's a great cook, though being a girl she doesn't know much about laptop computers and . . .'

'I know more than you do,' Mrs Marrell said, 'and I'm good with chainsaws, don't you forget it, but I don't mind bringing in cake and maybe, say, a bit of orange juice which is rich in vitamin C, so orange juice is good for children and for senior citizens too . . .'

As his granddaughter talked on, Old Baldy was standing aside and waving them into the hall. Still talking, she walked ahead of them then turned off to the left while Old Baldy, coming up behind them (hobbling a bit and yet still remarkably spry for a man who was over ninety), slid past them and then turned right, beckoning over his shoulder. 'Come on! Come on! Come on!' he was saying. 'This way! No need to worry . . . there's plenty of room. Come on!'

Ditta, holding the bag with Hilly's book in it, followed him. Max and Mirabel followed Ditta, Mirabel patting the pocket which held the disk in its clean envelope.

They came into a shady room, curtains half-drawn across windows that looked out onto a strip of lawn planted with three lemon trees.

At one end of the room was a big desk, drawers on either side of its knee-space, and a great many pigeonholes overflowing with various papers and old envelopes. In the middle of its flat top sat a small black laptop computer. A black cord trailed across the desk and down towards the wall, making it look even more like some sort of pet, kept safe on the end of a leash.

Max looked at the cord rather anxiously. 'We need to unplug your computer from the wall,' he said. 'Is it charged up? Does it run on batteries?'

'I take it into the park with me sometimes, don't I?' Old Baldy said indignantly. 'You've seen see me sitting there with it, haven't you? Where there isn't any wall and aren't any plugs, setting down my impressions of the world because the world doesn't hold still, you know. No way! It's always melting and changing and a man like me needs to set things down before — whoosh! — they' re gone for good and . . . what are you doing? What's that book you're putting down beside my computer?

'Hey willikins! That's a big book, that one . . . a lot of writing and reading in a book like that, isn't there? It would take even me (and I'm a quick reader) a year or two to get through a book as long as that even if it had pictures on every page, and . . .'

'This book,' said Ditta, 'this book is a haunted book. It's got a ghost in it.'

Old Baldy started back. 'Not another one,' he cried. 'One ghost is enough for any man, no matter if he lives to be a hundred or even a hundred and one . . .'

At that moment Hilly appeared, looking a lot brighter in the shady room than he had looked in the sunlight, and Old Baldy fell silent . . . though just for a second.

'A ghost!' he began. 'Another one! Listen, I told you I'm finished with ghosts . . . absolutely, utterly totally had enough of them . . . not that this one looks as if he'd be any trouble but all the same . . .'

'Have you ever heard the saying, *set a thief to catch a thief*?' asked Hilly quickly. 'Well, why not set a ghost to catch a ghost? If you want answers to ghost questions and mysteries a ghost is the one you should ask.'

Mirabel had been peering at the laptop. 'I don't know if it matters what program you're running when it comes to ghosts,' she said. 'Maybe ghosts just match up with any program. Anyhow, I'll disconnect it from the wall and we'll have a go. Are you sure?' she added, looking at Hilly.

'Of course I'm sure,' he said. 'It's great to be having an adventure. I mean I don't mind haunting the library but being out in the world again is just — well, it's just wonderful. And I do feel sorry for Max's ghost.'

'It's not my ghost,' said Max from somewhere behind them.

'You're right about being out in the world,' cried Old Baldy. 'I fancy being out in the world myself, though being out in the world takes it out of a man of my age . . . did I mention I'm over ninety? Which is getting on a bit, but I go to the park every day, rain or shine, particularly shine, of course, because when it's raining the sky drips . . . the trees drip and . . .'

He droned on as Mirabel, quick and sure, flipped the laptop open. A screen like a dark hand-mirror shone out and up at them. Mirabel pressed a button and, after thinking things over for a moment or two, the screen lit up and came alive. She slipped the disk into a slot in the front of the laptop and, as she did, Ditta and Max saw Hilly dissolving.

First his colours seemed to become watery and fade away into strange stains in the air, while his outline swam around its edges, then wavered off into nothing.

Old Baldy stopped talking and stared fixedly at the space Hilly had left behind him.

'Now that,' he said, 'that's something you don't see every day. In fact you don't even see it very often. In fact I don't know that I've ever seen it before . . . not quite like that, not in all my years . . . did I mention being over ninety?'

The laptop screen gave an electronic squeak and lit up. There was Hilly, a flat bright shape waving at them. His lips moved but they couldn't hear his voice. He turned and pointed downwards.

The laptop didn't have a mouse like Max's computer. There was a button in the middle of the keyboard and Mirabel took hold of it between the thumb and first two fingers of her right hand. She shifted it upwards, and when she did this Hilly's arm rose and pointed upwards too.

'I don't know,' muttered Mirabel to herself. It was as if she had forgotten Ditta, Max and Old Baldy were standing in the room behind her. 'Give it a go, I suppose, and then we'll see!'

Ditta thought Mirabel pressed something. A small menu shot up on the screen. Quickly Mirabel shifted the cursor, paused then pressed something again. Two heartbeats, and then once again that horrible oozing greenish colour erupted over the screen.

Hilly swayed to and fro like someone suddenly caught up in a loathsome storm. No one in the room could really feel the storm but they could see it raging in front of them and somehow the sight of its fury made them feel as if they were being tumbled over by it.

There were no speakers on the laptop, but suddenly words — fiery, furious words — began to appear across the bottom of the screen, crawling in from the left and disappearing to the right . . .

At last! At last! I will have my revenge! Yes, my revenge! They buried me there. They left me. They set off for home without me. But first they killed me. And now I will get my own back. Yes! You out there, now I will kill you. Kill you all! Kill the world.

CHAPTER 16

IT was horrible. Ditta stepped back, jostling Old Baldy and Max who were both stepping back.

But then words of a different size and shape appeared, chasing the first fiery words right off the screen.

But you can't kill me! I'm a ghost already . . . a ghost like you. I've come to talk to you. I've come to find out what happened to you and why you've been haunting my friend's floorboards.

The fiery words took over once more, running faster and faster, racing from left to right, burning across the screen as if, somewhere, invisible fingers were flickering madly across an invisible keyboard.

Years and year and years and years! Buried and left to rot. Fed to a tree. But I won! I turned into that tree and that tree turned into me. Then the wood became me and I became the wood. And later I was built into a wall.

And later, much later I was laid down as floor . . . a floor with people walking backwards and forwards over me in their filthy shoes.

But I wouldn't give in. I've never given in. Because they left me, those first ones, my shipmates. They left me behind. But more than that . . . more than that . . . more than that . . .

The words repeated themselves as if the furious ghost couldn't find the right words to say whatever it needed to say.

Yes . . . go on, tell me, said the line of print that was Hilly's voice.

The ghost's words seemed to explode on the screen.

They killed me. Young Garibaldi, he killed

me. And the others . . . they were all on his side. They rallied around him. They kept his secret. Standing around my body they plotted to hide what he'd done. They all agreed to tell the captain I'd fallen.

The words were still furious, and yet, as the ghost began telling its story, somehow the green storm beating in on Hilly seemed to be lessening. He was still staggering on the screen as if he were struggling against the horrible wind, but for all that he seemed to be standing just a little stronger and straighter.

The print faded away. A new line appeared.

Hilly was speaking again. *I know what that's like,* he was saying — or that's what his words, running across the bottom of the screen, were saying. *I fell too. And falling killed me.*

There was a sudden change in the light coming from the screen. The green colour became somehow softer. It stopped its seething and bubbling. It grew still. And suddenly the greenness seemed to fall in on itself.

There, before their eyes a new shape was forming, and Hilly was no longer the only figure on the screen. Bit by bit, a tall man appeared beside him, standing over and looking down at him . . . a man dressed in an old-fashioned jacket and a peaked hat.

His lips moved. *You say you fell too?* his line of print inquired.

I was reading this book, said Hilly.

He held up the ghost of the blue book that was sitting solidly beside Baldy's laptop.

The story was so exciting . . . you know how it is with some stories . . . you just have to know what happens next. But my mother was after me. 'Stop that reading!' she told me. Then 'Bring in some wood for the fire.' Then 'Get that broom from by the window. Sweep the hearth!' Because this was in the days before there were such things as vacuum cleaners . . .

His line of print was interrupted.

The ghost was impatient.

VACUUM CLEANERS! WHAT ARE YOU ON ABOUT? WHY ARE YOU TALKING NONSENSE TO ME?

The fiery letters burned for a moment.

Hilly's line of print took over, calmly and firmly.

Never mind! I was just mentioning a change in the world since the days of brooms. The thing was I wanted to finish my book. That was all that mattered, back then. So I thought I'd climb the tree and get up onto the roof. It was a sunny day and I loved the thought of being high above everything else, reading away with no one telling me what to do next.

And when my mother was busy with the baby I slipped outside, taking my book with me. I began to climb. Up and up, I went branch to branch. And then just as I was clambering onto the roof I dropped the book.

'Oh no!' exclaimed a voice. Ditta was so startled she tore her eyes from the screen to glance left and right, only to find Max and Mirabel looking at her. The voice she had heard crying out had been her own, pushing its way through fingers she had clapped across her mouth. Quickly she looked back at the little screen.

I tried to catch it, Hilly's line of print was saying. *I missed it. The book fell. And I fell. I remember falling, hitting branches on the way down. One branch smashed against my head. I remember that so clearly. It was just as if my head turned into a drum with someone beating out a great, single stroke down on it.*

I lay on the grass beneath the tree and my book was only a few inches away from me. I put out my hand to touch it and . . .'

For a moment the line of print broke off.

And? said the ghost's line of print, appearing as Hilly's last words faded away.

. . . and the next thing I was somehow inside the book, looking out at myself, all limp on the grass . . . looking out as my mother came racing out of the house, and knelt beside me, and wept, and called me her darling boy, and tried to wake me up again.

But by then I was a ghost haunting the book I never finished.

The other line of print took over.

I understand all that, it said, and by now the print was definitely less furious, less fiery. There was certainly a calmer, more even look to the letters.

In a way it was like that with me. We'd gone ashore searching for fresh water . . . getting some idea of the lie of the new land. We were all excited at being ashore, after all those weeks and weeks and weeks at sea, and some of the lads were a bit on the lively side.

Over-vigorous, you might say. They wasn't too keen on me as an h'officer either. Because

(if I'm honest) I was sterner than most. Well, to be extra-honest I was rough on the deckhands. Unkind beyond the call of duty. I'd come up the hard way myself, d'ye see?

I know they were hard times for a lot of people. In the school library I was able to go in and out of a few history books when people left them near the dictionaries, and I know those past times could be really hard times.

Hard? Yes, hard! People today, why, they'd shiver if they knew about the hardness back then. But even so, I might have overdone it. I might have been harder than necessary even for tough times.

Anyhow that young Garibaldi — he was a bit slow to do something I told him to do, and I swung at him. Smacked him really hard. I think, looking back, I might have broken his nose.

And he — well, he was a tough young man and we were up on the hill — on the edge of a little cliff as it happened. I think that, being on land again, it seemed to young Garibaldi that he was in another world altogether from the world of the ship he'd been on a couple of hours back.

Anyhow he hauled around and hit me back. I toppled sideways . . . slipped . . . fell like you . . . crash, crash, crash . . . down onto the rocks below, and there I lay. Bleeding and broken beyond what any doctor could put together again.

Well, there was nowhere for those sailors to go but back to the ship, and nothing for it but to tell the captain what they had to tell. But the men, all seven of them, agreed to protect young Garibaldi by saying I'd gone over under my own steam.

Nothing about anyone hitting me. Oh no! One and all they declared it was all my own fault. And in due course the ship's crew buried me there, and said a few prayers over me along with a civil word or two. Polite enough, but not said out of true friendship.

At least they could have named that hill after me — Blake was my name back when I had a name — Blake's Hill they could have called it, but no! When the maps were drawn that hill was named after Captain Croyden . . . Croyden's Hill.

They planted a little tree on my grave before they set sail back to the Motherland,

and I was left behind. Not even a name over me . . . all on my own . . . with the tree growing down into me, its roots feeding and feeling around my bones, eating me up, me and my name both.

Left behind. Left behind!

The print sparked and glowed as if it might be going to catch fire again, but Hilly's print cut across it.

That's the way of the world. No way out of it. Things are always changing. The egg changes into the bird. Men and women spring up, then fall back again and with a bit of luck become good green grass. Except some of us turn into ghosts. For instance I haunt the book. And you haunted the tree. And then when the tree was cut down you haunted the wood of the tree. And then, because you were a clever ghost, you found your way into that computer.

For a moment no print appeared on the screen. The children stared at Hilly and the man in the peaked cap. They could see their lips moving and their eyes blinking but there was no sound. Then the sailor's print appeared, smoky now, rather than fiery.

I've had time to think about it over the

*years. And though for the most part I
roared and ranted first inside the tree, then
inside the wood, I've spent a bit of time
remembering.*

*Remembering that last moment, like
you remember falling from the tree. And
remembering I was rough on those men.
Rough beyond the call of duty. Rough on the
one who struck back at me.*

*Sometimes I've almost wanted to ask his
pardon. Not often, because he got his own
back, didn't he? Because I was left . . . left
behind . . . left alone.*

The letters twisted and began to glow once
more. But Hilly's letters raced onto the screen,
becoming even more powerful.

*Now listen! Just listen! You're a man with
a story to tell. And you need to tell that story.
Because maybe telling the story will lift the
loneliness away from you.*

*Oh, I've got a story to tell all right, but
who'd listen? I've tried to tell my tale,
twisting in the wood year after year. I've
tried to tell it. But no one lends an ear. They
all hate me too much.*

They don't hate you — the ones out there.

They don't even know who you are. But when the wood twists at night . . . when it seethes and moans . . . that frightens people, so they're far too scared to sit around listening for the next bit. You see, you're in another time these days, and you've got me. I'm here listening. So you can tell me your whole story. Not just the bits you've told me so far, but the whole thing, starting from the beginning, and adding in the details . . . what sort of day it was, that day? What did you think of the new place you were in and what did you actually say to young Garibaldi to set off the fight? You can tell me everything! And — well, I don't know, but there are people out there clever with machines like this one. Maybe they can catch your story and print it out. It may become part of history.

History . . . History! Now there's a word with a bit of a taste to it. You think I might turn out to be part of history after all?

You already are. So am I. It's not so bad. And even the ones out there looking in at us at this very moment . . . they're part of history too, even if their particular history is so very new.

There's a second of Now (the present, that is) which becomes, almost at once, a second of

Then (that's the past). And every second of the past is history.

But not too many people can tell about it the way ghosts can. So when someone knows your history — sets it down — puts it in a library maybe, well, you're part of the world. You'll be remembered and thought about. You'll never be alone again.

All right, said the ghost.

It was easy to imagine, from the look of his laptop print, that he was speaking eagerly.

When shall I begin my telling?

We both belong to the past, and there's no time like the past. But there's no time like the present either. Begin now.

Ditta and Max, Mirabel and Old Baldy were all staring at the screen as fixed as people of stone, but then the door opened behind them.

Old Baldy's granddaughter came in with a wide tray so loaded down she could hardly carry it. On the tray was a jug of apple juice and a teapot, a small jug of milk, cups and glasses piled inside one another and a plate overflowing with huge slices of cake.

'What are you watching?' she asked. 'One of those sea stories is it? He loves his sea stories, and no wonder, coming from a family of sailors the way we do, because his own great-grandfather, my own great-great-grandfather, if I've got it worked out right, was a sailor, you know, and came out here ages back in the early days . . .'

'I'll tell them that story,' cried Old Baldy, cutting in quickly. 'You don't have to say a word. But first we'll tuck into this cake. She makes great cake, this girl here. And she's like me, a citizen of the times, because she can change the tyre on a truck and, as I mentioned earlier, she can make good use of one of those chainsaws, which we didn't have in the past. Oh no, it was backwards and forwards with us when we was sawing wood, which we had to do a lot of, backwards and forwards . . . backwards and forwards, this way and that way . . . the saw biting down into the wood . . .'

'I expect she would have been a great sailor too, back in the old days,' said Ditta in a respectful voice, but still watching words come and go on the screen, line after line as stories went backwards and forwards between Hilly and the sailor ghost.

Mirabel was crouched over the keyboard

pressing the *Save* key every now and then.

I'll be able to print it all out later, Ditta was thinking.

'No doubt I really would have made a great sailor all right, if they'd let girls go to sea back then,' said Mrs Marrell. 'Because, like I was saying, I come from a sea-going family. And we've got a lot of sailor ancestors between us, him and me.'

CHAPTER 17

'DITTA! Max! This is just wonderful,' said their teacher Mrs Prentice in a highly respectful voice, rare in teachers. 'You've done some really good research.'

Ditta and Max looked modestly at their feet. 'Really good research,' repeated Mrs Prentice. 'But there's more to it than that. While I'm reading what you've written it's almost as if I'm living through your story . . . and it's a dramatic story too. Of course you've obviously made parts of it up. But you've really got the feeling of what it must have been like to live and work on a sailing ship back in 1800 — what did you read? Where did you do your research?'

Max and Ditta stopped looking at their feet and looked at each other.

'We started working in the library,' said Ditta. 'There are a lot of reference books in that corner close to the stationery cupboards. We got to know the library really well,' she added.

'We've turned into class librarians,' said Max. 'We help Mrs Carmody every afternoon after school.'

'Well I'm going to photocopy this project of yours,' said Mrs Prentice. 'I'm going to run off several copies — one for the staffroom, and a copy for the library, and your parents would probably like to have copies too. We'll put it with the other reference books . . . in that corner that's always flickering with shadows . . . and then the other children will be able to use it. And I know teachers will want to read it. It's just so good.' She hesitated. 'Just promise me you didn't copy it all out of some other book.'

'We didn't!' cried Ditta rather indignantly. 'We just — we just did research.'

'Good research!' Max added. 'It was really hard, but it helped us to imagine what it would be like to be at sea in those days.'

'We imagined it and then we put it onto the computer and printed it out,' Ditta said, and of course this was partly true. *But*, Ditta was thinking, *if we told Mrs Prentice the whole truth about our research she wouldn't believe us anyway. Teachers sometimes need to be protected from the truth.*

Later that day she sat in the red chair in Max's room. Mirabel sat hunched on the office chair in front of the computer and Max slumped on his bed. Bosun Blake shimmered on the screen in front of them and Hilly stood by the window holding his book, wavering just a little in the breeze that was stirring the curtains.

'I expect Old Baldy's on his way to the park,' said Hilly, staring out through the window. 'It's great there, out in the sun with the sound of the sea coming in across town. But maybe we should ask Old Baldy into our meeting?'

'There isn't any room for anyone else,' said

Ditta. 'We'll put him down as a consultant. We don't need to ask his permission. Old Baldy's the sort of man who always loves to be consulted.' She scribbled in her folder.

'And later on we'll set off for the park ourselves and tell him what's been happening. Well, if there's time we will because you need a lot of time for an Old Baldy consultation.'

She took out a printed page, held it up and looked around the edge of it. 'Ready?' She read aloud in her best executive voice. 'This is the first meeting . . . the first official meeting, that is . . . of Mystic Investigators Incorporated.'

Max groaned. 'What are you on about?' he cried. 'What do you mean *Incorporated*? Let's get outside and do something.'

'No listen . . . listen!' shouted Ditta. 'Don't you see? We're doing something. We know a lot of things no one else knows. We've got specialist information between us. And we can kick off a really good business with what we know. Maybe we could charge fees . . . make money.'

Max sat down again, rather quickly.

'Money?' he asked. 'How?'

'We've solved the ghost problem of your room,' said Ditta. 'You haven't had any more trouble with your floor, have you?'

'That he hasn't!' Blake's voice came drifting out through the computer speakers. 'I'm not going back into those floorboards, not ever again. Not likely. That computer disk is really comfortable after what I've had to put up with over the last two hundred years.

'It's small but I can curl up in it, like a cat curls up. I can slip out onto the screen when you call me up and cast a weather eye over the outside world, and then, in between times, I can sleep. Now I'm part of a crew again I can treat that disk as my hammock and rest in it. Maybe with a bit of true rest I'll learn to be a better man.'

Ditta nodded at Blake, then turned to Max. She counted on her fingers. 'There's you and me, Max. Then there's Mirabel . . . I know she's irritating but she's great with computers. And now we've got Hilly and Blake. Two ghosts. And who would know more about ghosts than ghosts themselves? They can be our specialist consultants.'

'Specialists?' said Max. 'Consultants? What are you on about?'

'I've told you. Mystic Investigators Incorporated!' declared Ditta waving the page at him. 'Mirabel will set up a web page, and we'll offer to help anyone who has a haunted house. There must be a few other haunted houses out there. It'll be our after-school job.'

Max looked suddenly interested.

'You mean we could get paid for it?' His face cleared. 'Hey! You're right. We could, you know. There was that film *Ghostbusters*. We could . . .'

'Listen, matey, I'm not having anything to do with busting another ghost,' cried Blake. 'Ghosts need understanding, not busting.'

'Some of them might need busting,' Max argued. Blake puffed up and began to turn slightly green. 'All right! All right!' cried Max quickly. 'They need understanding too. But with you and Hilly we could be Ghostunderstanders, couldn't we? OK. Let's start a business. I'll be president.'

'No, I'm president already,' said Ditta. 'You can be vice president but you've got to be a lot of other things too. You can bike so quickly you'd better be our messenger.'

'I think I could help him invent a ghost detector,' said Hilly, 'because, face it, not all ghosts are like me. I mean you lot can see me,

172

but a lot of people can't. And Max's parents couldn't even feel the floor twist or hear it moan . . .'

'They knew I was there, though,' said Blake. 'In a way they knew I was there. They felt uncomfortable at times, uncomfortable without knowing why. But you're right, matey! Maybe we could come up with something — some device that would force wicked ghosts — really wicked ghosts, that is — to show themselves so we could deal with them according to what seemed proper.'

'Not that we want to be treacherous to other ghosts,' Hilly added quickly, 'but maybe we could help them. After all, we helped Blake.'

'True! True!' said Blake. 'I was done to death . . . but that's all in the past. I'm willing to forgive and forget . . .well, I am forgiving and forgetting, aren't I . . . and that's because you set me free.'

Mirabel's fingers flitted over the keyboard.

'I've got something to show you,' she said. 'Look here!' The screen split in two. Blake was crowded in the left-hand side. Names and phone numbers began to scroll down the other half of the screen.

'Last night before I went to bed,' she said, 'I put out a query on the Internet. *Are you bothered with ghosts? Can we help you?* And look. One . . . two . . . three . . . eleven names and phone numbers. Eleven people say they're being haunted and they need help.'

They all stared at the screen.

'It's probably the ghosts that really need help,' said Hilly. 'They're probably even more troubled than the people complaining about them. And Blake and I ought to help them.'

'We can help them,' said Ditta. She was becoming more and more certain they were on to a winner. 'We can help everyone. Hilly and Blake can help the haunters, and we can help the haunted ones. Do you all agree?'

Hilly nodded slowly. On the screen Blake was nodding. After a pause, Max nodded as well. Only Mirabel hesitated.

'Mirabel?' said Ditta.

'What?' said Mirabel, seeming to wake out of a dream.

'Do you want to be computer adviser in a ghost research business?'

'Oh that,' said Mirabel. 'I thought it was all done with. Yes, of course!'

Happiness and hope flooded through Ditta. 'Right then!' she cried. 'We're in business. Now to put things in order. Number one . . .'

Maddigan's Quest
Margaret Mahy

I don't know if the world counts as the world any more, not since the wars of the Destruction . . . we're the leftover people going between the leftover places.

In a time not far from our own, a colourful group of travellers brave the twisting, tricksy landscape of the Remaking, after Chaos ripped the world apart. They are the magicians, clowns, trapeze artists and musicians of Maddigan's Fantasia, healing the injured land with their gifts of wonder and laughter.

Garland Maddigan, the 12-year-old daughter of Ferdy, the Fantasia's ringmaster, has made the trip before, but this journey offers frightening new challenges. Three mysterious children join the Fantasia and the sinister strangers who follow them become a dangerous enigma as Garland slowly unlocks their secret origin.

HarperCollins*Publishers*